Philip and Faith:
A Tale of
Development

by

Terry Wright

 New Generation Publishing

'In a higher world it is otherwise; but here below to live is to change, and to be perfect is to have changed often.'

John Henry Newman, *An Essay on the Development of Christian Doctrine*

Contents

Prologue (2010)

'What time does it start?'

Philip was munching his toast while contemplating a photograph of Pope Benedict on the front page of the newspaper on his kitchen table. He wasn't too keen on the German Pope, whose persecution of liberal theologians while he was still Cardinal Ratzinger, Head of the Sacred Congregation of the Doctrine of the Faith, had earned him the soubriquet 'the Pope's Rottweiler'. Since he had become Pope, however, even Philip had to admit, he had shown more restraint and on this visit to Britain, which was to reach its climax with the beatification of John Henry Newman, he had behaved more like a favourite grandfather than a pontiff. The press were now chucking him under the chin (the etymological meaning of the word soubriquet, as Philip was fond of pointing out) as if he were a pet cat rather than one of the most powerful men on earth.

It was to the beatification ceremony in Birmingham, to be covered live on television, that Philip was referring, as Faith immediately realised.

'At eleven, I think,' she replied.

Faith was visiting for the weekend, taking a break from her duties at the parish in County Durham whose vicar she had recently been appointed. Although he argued vociferously in favour of his own Catholic Church accepting women priests, Philip hadn't in practice grown used to the idea of his former girlfriend being ordained. Faith might be approaching sixty but he still found her attractive, still saw in her aspects of the teenage girl with whom he had fallen in love so many years earlier.

'I expect the television coverage will have started already,' Philip continued. 'It's a bit like the Cup Final: you have to watch the build-up to the event itself, the teams leaving their hotel and boarding the coach, the fans trudging to the ground, the pundits pondering the likely outcome and interviews with key players. Cofton Park sounds as if it should be a football ground anyway. Let's see how far they've got.'

They moved through to the living room where Philip switched on the television. Sure enough, there were the pilgrims, making their way through wind and rain to the park. A commentator was explaining that this was the first ever beatification to take place on English soil and that it was one hundred and twenty years after the great man's death. Philip couldn't help adding his own comments.

'Of course, if he had been a French peasant having visions of the Virgin Mary he would have been beatified within a few years but an intellectual, struggling heroically to make sense of his faith in the modern world – that takes over a century.'

'Well, he wasn't that heroic,' Faith insisted. 'All he did was take a long time to change his mind. And don't prospective saints need a miracle of some sort before they can be beatified?'

'Yes, and that has been one of his difficulties. The Friends of Cardinal Newman, who are promoting his cause, have been crying out for ages for people to report something miraculous. Their newsletter is full of children reporting help with their exams – an appropriate enough activity, I suppose, for an academic saint. But now they've managed to find an American deacon with a dodgy back who claimed to have been cured after invoking Newman in prayer.'

'Does that count?'

'Apparently so. The Church has quite rigorous

requirements, involving two doctors who vouch for the inexplicability of the cure, medically speaking.'

'But I thought backs were notoriously mysterious.'

'They are. I don't really care about the American's back and I'd be surprised if the Vatican does either. They want a good role model and Newman fits the bill, at least their version of Newman'.

'*Their version?*'

'Well, Newman is difficult to label. Progressives and traditionalists, liberals and conservatives, whatever you want to call them, have been arguing over Newman for ages, both sides claiming him as theirs. With a careful selection of quotations you can make him support almost anything. At the moment the Vatican are picking out the 'anti-liberal' citations, like his Biglietto speech on becoming a Cardinal. If you go back to the previous decade, the beginning of the 1860s, you could find some bitter comments on papal power. You won't hear any of those quoted today!'

'Oh, I see.' Faith didn't really see but she knew better than to question Philip too closely once he got onto one of his hobby horses.

'Oh my God, it's Edward!' Philip shouted, pointing at the screen. 'He used to supervise me. He must be in his late sixties and he still has a baby face under that imposing beard. I should have known they would turn to him for expert comment. And that's Father Sean with him. He was the Catholic Chaplain at Oxford when I converted. He's now principal of some college in Rome.'

Philip focussed more intently at the screen, intrigued to know how the two academics would adapt to their new role. Both were having some difficulty in being heard over the background noise, a combination of loudspeaker announcements and a large choir beneath a massive canvas tent erected for the occasion.

'Do you remember 1966?' Faith asked.

'You mean the World Cup?'

'No, you fool, the Billy Graham crusade. I sang in the choir, if you remember. We hadn't met then but you've told me that you went forward at one of the meetings.'

'I did but I try not to remember.' Philip was genuinely embarrassed to recall how he had first come to faith. It wasn't altogether respectable in intellectual circles to admit to any sort of faith, let alone an evangelical one.

The singing from Cofton Park, however, as at the crusade so many years before, was quite impressive. The television coverage now switched to the arrival of the papal helicopter from which a smiling Pope Benedict soon emerged. He then mounted into his specially made Popemobile before gradually making his way through the crowd to the central stage at which the mass was going to be celebrated. It was over thirty years now since Philip had been received into the Catholic Church but he still found it hard to share the enthusiasm that cradle-Catholics had for their leader. He watched incredulously as Pope Benedict passed through the cheering crowd, pausing to kiss the occasional child and to wave to his adoring admirers.

'I think it's rather nice that they love him so much,' Faith observed. 'He's the descendant of Peter after all.'

'You're not supposed to believe that,' Philip objected.

'Why not, so long as he's only "first among equals"?'

'Equals, my arse!'

'I don't see what your arse has to do with it.' Faith had always disliked the vehemence with which Philip sometimes expressed himself while Philip often felt she was too prim and proper. That had been one of the reasons for their relationship foundering so many years earlier.

On screen a prominent ecclesiastical historian was attempting to make himself heard over the noise of the loudspeakers. But the Popemobile had by now reached the stage and preparations were under way for the mass itself. The crowd subsided into reverent silence. Philip and Faith too settled down to watch the proceedings with only the occasional comment punctuating their silence.

Chapter 1

Epistle

That evening, after Faith had returned to her parish, Philip decided to check the newsreel footage of Billy Graham's Crusade on the internet later that day. The black and white images quickly triggered his own memories of the occasion. It had been about a month before the start of the World Cup finals when he had been persuaded to attend the crusade by some evangelicals in his class. It had also been the summer of his 'O' levels so he might have been better advised to have spent the evening revising. But he had been intrigued by the posters advertising the return of the clean-cut farmer's son from North Carolina who had made such a big impact on his previous London crusade in 1954. Any chance to escape the confines of his school in south London, where he was one of only a few boarders, was always welcome. So he and his friend Michael, a fellow-boarder, had agreed to join the small band of evangelicals making their way to Earl's Court.

Michael, like Philip, was an Army child, forced either to follow his father across the globe to whichever remaining corner of the Empire he was posted or to be packed off to boarding school. In Michael's case there was the added complication that his mother had recently died of cancer. Philip had made a particular effort to befriend him although they had little in common apart from their military background and a keen interest in football. They would occasionally travel together to watch Chelsea or West Ham, the teams they supported, since London was only a brief train journey away. They saw this trip to hear Billy

Graham as another opportunity to escape the monotony of school routine

Earl's Court was as easy to reach as Stamford Bridge – just a few stops along the District line from Victoria – and they soon emerged blinking in the evening sunlight, joining the crowds making their way into the arena. It was like going to watch Chelsea in other respects too; there were the same coaches, the same police horses patrolling the crowds, even if the excitement of the 'supporters' was more subdued. 'Ticket Holders Only', it said on a banner outside the hall, reinforcing the similarity to match days. Philip kept this comparison to himself, however, not wanting to offend his evangelical companions, who had by now entered the arena and were hurrying upstairs to their seats in the gallery.

The sight that greeted them from the gallery was impressive: three large blocks of seats in the centre of the hall stretching out towards a platform at the front on which a huge choir, all with white shirts or blouses, was singing. Behind them on the far wall a fluttering white banner proclaimed, 'I am the Way, the Truth and the Life'. Philip had been prepared to be sceptical, as his Religious Studies teacher had said he should, but he couldn't help being impressed by the swelling chorus, 'How great thou art, how great thou art'. He turned to Michael to acknowledge his appreciation of the singing. The choir was so loud, however, that it was hard to keep a conversation going, so they both sat back and allowed the music to wash over them.

After several more hymns the director of the choir turned to address the audience. He was clearly the warm-up man, welcoming them all to the meeting and asking those who had never been to a crusade before to wave their programmes in the air. Philip rolled his eyes at Michael in silent protest and kept his programme firmly in his pocket. There were some introductory prayers by local clergy and a few more hymns before Billy Graham finally made his entrance, striding confidently to the platform. He looked exactly as he did on the posters, with his strong, jutting jaw and glowing face beneath neatly-brushed waves of hair. He began gently, saying how pleased he was to be here and making a joke or two about London. On his last visit, back in 1954, he recalled, he had made a disastrous trip to Soho, wanting to show that God loved everyone, even the most hardened sinner. But he had been made to beat a hasty retreat, driven back by a combination of women revealing more than he wanted to see and their potential clients, impatient to be left alone. He hadn't made the same mistake this time although his message, he insisted, remained the same: however sinful and unworthy you felt yourself to be, it was never too late to turn to God.

He was getting into his stride now, his voice rising and his delivery gathering pace as he turned to what he called 'the terrible fact of sin'. Philip had been warned that the sermon would be heavy on sin, battering the audience into recognition of their guilt before holding out the prospect of redemption. He hadn't reckoned, however, with the vehemence of the attack on the modern world and its 'rebellion' against God or with so many examples of celebrities who had spent their lives in the pursuit of pleasure only to end in despair and loneliness. They included pop singers who had overdosed on drugs, politicians whose corruption had been dramatically revealed, and writers who could find nothing worth living for.

Philip began to feel distinctly uncomfortable, shifting on his plastic chair as the evangelist's voice rose in protest against what St.Paul had called 'spiritual wickedness in high places'. This, he joked, didn't simply mean that the Archbishop of Canterbury wasn't as good as he made out. No, it was worse than that because, as St.Peter had warned, 'the devil, as a roaring lion, walketh about, seeking whom he may devour.' The atmosphere of the hall grew distinctly hotter as the preacher warmed to his task, convincing his audience of the predominance of sin in the world. He painted a devastating picture of the sheer hopelessness of a world without the saving grace of Jesus Christ. And that was where the tone of the sermon changed, for there was, it seemed, a solution to all these terrible problems. If we turned back to God, as revealed through Christ, if we repented of all our wickedness, there was a possibility of salvation, of being redeemed from this slavery to sin.

Now came the positive part of the message, focussing on the man from Galilee, his life and teaching, his death and resurrection. It was the same message, Billy Graham insisted, as that which St.Paul had preached in the middle of the first century, how Christ's sacrifice upon the cross was a revelation of God's love while his resurrection promised final victory over evil. Simply by turning to him, following his example and trusting in his grace, we could escape from despair, loneliness and anxiety. Philip could sense the atmosphere in the auditorium changing, the mood lightening as Billy Graham told them all how much God loved them and wanted them to return His love. He was longing for them to turn to Him. It didn't matter what they had done; He would forgive them. Now was the chance to turn their lives around, to repent, to change direction. They just needed a small push and that was what he wanted to supply: 'I am going to ask you to get up out of your seat right now and come to the front.' This would be the start of a long journey; they would say a prayer together and then each of them would be seen by a counsellor, who would give them some 'devotional literature'. Philip had heard that the evening ended this way, that something like a thousand people 'committed themselves to Christ' each night. He had certainly not anticipated becoming one of them himself but something inside was urging him to go forward.

Philip glanced at Michael beside him. He too seemed to be in the grip of conflicting emotions. All around them others were getting out of their seats and making their way to the front. Philip decided that he must answer what seemed like a call; he must acknowledge this deep longing within himself. He got up clumsily and shuffled along the row to the aisle. Michael, he noticed, had followed and the two made their way downstairs, joining a stream of people making their way to the front where Billy Graham himself stood with his head bowed, praying in silence. There was now quite a crowd of people gathered around him.

What happened next was a bit hazy in Philip's mind at a distance of over forty years. Billy Graham had said a prayer with them, he remembered, exhorting them all to remain faithful, then they had been ushered to a room elsewhere in the building and assigned to a counsellor. In Philip's case this proved to be a pale, rather intense young man dressed in a grey suit, who thrust a pack of the promised 'devotional literature' into his hand and talked earnestly to him for about twenty minutes, mainly about his own conversion some years earlier and how difficult he had found it to sustain his faith without belonging to a community of believers. Philip, who was by now anxious to get away, to reflect by himself on what had happened, listened in rather resentful silence. He was already beginning to doubt the reality of the 'call' he had received. Where had it come from? Was it simply from his own emotional need? And how could one possibly tell?

Finally released, Philip noticed Michael still engaged in earnest conversation with another counsellor. So he waited for them to finish, leafing through the 'literature' he had been given. Before he could explore it properly, however, he noticed that Michael too was now free. The two of them hurried from the room, comparing notes on what their counsellors had said.

'What was your guy like?' Philip asked.

'A bit of a prat, to be honest.' 'Mine too. He was probably some kind of bank clerk, to judge by his suit.'

Whatever else Philip's call had produced, it didn't seem to have done much for his generosity of spirit. Neither he nor Michael wanted to talk much about what they had felt, whatever it was that had compelled them to go forward. What they most dreaded was meeting up again with their companions. Unfortunately, they found them waiting on the platform at Earl's Court, where the two 'converts' were greeted with effusive congratulations. Looking back at his adolescent self from a distance of over forty years, it seemed strange that he should have felt so embarrassed by it all. Was his memory playing tricks, reading back later emotions into the original event? He didn't think so; even at sixteen, his mind and his heart seemed to have been struggling against each other. Part of him wanted to believe everything he had been told but another part reserved judgment, already beginning to ask questions.

Philip remembered vividly the dread he felt about what people would say in the boarding house when they returned and news of their 'conversion' became public. Sure enough, Ian, a self-consciously intellectual sixth-former, sought Philip out the following evening and grilled him about what had happened:

'You know what Billy Graham does; he makes you

feel as gloomy as possible about yourself and the state of the world and then, just when you can't stand any more, he offers you a way out.'

'What if that way works?' Philip replied. 'What if it is true?'

'What is truth?'

'Said jesting Pilate and would not wait for an answer.' Philip was pleased to have remembered this quotation from an essay by Bacon they had recently studied in class but Ian quickly resumed his attack.

'Look at Michael. He's obviously vulnerable, longing for some good news to counterbalance his recent loss.'

'Don't you dare say that to Michael himself,' Philip warned. He was seriously concerned that his friend would buckle under the weight of such taunts. Ian agreed to go easy on him but his eye was caught by the pack of 'devotional literature' which Philip was reading.

'What have you got in those papers, anyway?' he asked, snatching it away, opening it at random, and starting to read: 'Fill your name in the blanks in the following passages: "God so loved [blank] that he gave his only begotten Son that [blank] should not perish but have everlasting life." Talk about indoctrination!'

Philip snatched the papers back. He felt ashamed at the crudeness of their teaching methods but he was damned if he was going to admit it. He wondered if it was worth complaining about being bullied but realised that the housemaster would be unlikely to become involved in a dispute over religion. He was happy enough to preside over house prayers at the end of each day but the fact that two of his boys took them seriously would be a matter of embarrassment to him. And that, Philip quickly realised, was the attitude of most of the staff. The boys, however, were less reticent;

those who belonged to the Christian Union went out of their way to be friendly while others were quite openly scornful.

Philip and Michael both began meeting members of the Christian Union every day before school for prayer in the classroom of a sympathetic teacher. Philip recalled surprising even himself by being something of a star at extemporary prayer, talking to the Lord with a fluency which (at the time) he took as a sign of grace. He felt himself transported to another dimension of being. The words came spouting from him as if it were another Pentecost. Michael, in contrast, took a back seat at these meetings, less certain about his new faith. A similar difference between them was apparent in their modes of 'bearing witness' when they were asked to talk openly to a meeting of the Christian Union about their conversion. Philip quickly adopted the vocabulary of other evangelicals while Michael stumbled over his words, clearly uncomfortable with the whole process.

The pack of 'literature' which Philip and Michael had been given included a copy of one of Billy Graham's books, *Peace with God*, which they both read. Philip noticed that the biblical text most frequently invoked in it was the Epistle to the Romans so he suggested to Michael that they might study this together. Their Religious Studies teacher confirmed that it was one of the earliest attempts to summarise Christian belief and was therefore well worth grappling with. He warned them, however, that it would not make easy reading and recommended a commentary by William Barclay to help place it in context.

Reading this brief but complex letter, Philip recalled, was his first real experience of Christianity as a 'fact in the world's history' (to use a phrase he would later encounter in Newman). He learnt from Barclay's commentary that St.Paul's Letter to the Romans could be dated to the late 50s AD, after the Jews (including those now calling themselves Christians) had been allowed to return to the city of Rome following their expulsion by the Emperor Claudius a few years earlier. St.Paul was hoping to visit Rome on his way to preaching the gospel in Spain. The Christian community there, as in Jerusalem, was unsure how much of the Jewish Law needed to be retained; they wondered, for example, whether they should insist on circumcision for gentile converts.

Circumcision wasn't the easiest subject for Philip and Michael to discuss. They were even more embarrassed by St.Paul's attack on homosexuality at the end of the first chapter, where he talked of the wrath of God reserved for those who 'burned in their lust one toward another'. Being boarders at a school exclusively for boys, they didn't really have much choice about the objects of their affection. Philip had already had crushes on a number of other boys, normally blonde, pretty ones, which he would later call 'substitute girls'. He hadn't as yet acted upon these feelings; he wasn't even sure what homosexuals did to one another sexually. Hoping for an explanation of St.Paul's focus on this issue from Barclay, he read that Roman society was so 'riddled with unnatural vice' that fourteen out of the first fifteen Roman Emperors had been homosexuals. That would have made some rugby team, he told Michael, and they began speculating who the sole straight one had been.

In other ways the commentary was quite helpful, explaining some of the metaphors behind the doctrines of justification, atonement and redemption as St.Paul was trying to puzzle them out. Philip found the concept of atonement, the idea of God the Father requiring the sacrifice of his Son as a kind of scapegoat for the sins of His people, hard to fathom. But it began to make sense in the context of earlier Jewish practice. Redemption too became a more vivid concept when seen in the context of the freeing of slaves. They both found the middle chapters of the letter hard going. It took a leap of the historical imagination to cast themselves in the position of the early Christians, trying to work out their relationship to the Jewish Law.

Philip remembered being struck by some passages later on in the letter. That section in chapter eight, for example, enumerating all the things that couldn't separate us from the love of God. He couldn't fathom why angels should want to separate us from God but he read in Barclay that they were believed by the Jews to have a grudge against human beings, God's later creation. Even at the age of sixteen Philip could see that some of St.Paul's beliefs were distinctly of his time. His political philosophy in particular, recommending obedience to all authority because 'the powers that be are ordained of God', seemed rather naïve.

'I don't think you're supposed to say things like that about St.Paul,' Michael ventured.

'Why not?'

'It's the Bible, for God's sake. You're supposed to take what it says as gospel.'

'Says who?'

'Says Billy Graham for a start and all the people at the Christian Union.'

'Well, maybe they're wrong,' Philip insisted.

Recalling this exchange over forty years later, Philip couldn't help marvelling at the sheer confidence of his youthful self. But he also recalled having found the whole exercise of trying to reconstruct the historical context of the letter very rewarding. It was probably the first occasion in his life in which he had committed himself to genuine intellectual engagement with a text outside the school curriculum. Michael had been somewhat less enthusiastic; he also began extricating himself from the activities of the Christian Union. Philip on the other hand continued to play an important part in them. He became increasingly aware that his own attitudes didn't exactly chime in with those of the longer-serving members, who spoke much more reverently about the Bible as 'the Word of God'. Philip would point out the astonishing range of genres within it, from Job berating God for the suffering and injustice in the world to Solomon (or whoever wrote his song) going into raptures about his mistress's breasts. But it seemed to make no difference at all to the way they read it.

Philip was perhaps fortunate that the school provided him with the freedom to develop his own ideas at his own pace. Societies like the Christian Union were largely unsupervised; there was a master 'in charge' but he didn't normally attend meetings. In hindsight, however, Philip realised that he could have done with rather more guidance. If he had belonged to a church in the world outside the school, there would have been older, wiser members of the congregation to whom he could have turned for advice. If he had returned to some 'normal' community in the summer holidays rather than the army base in Singapore where his parents lived, there might have been adults with whom he could have discussed his new faith. But his parents were hostile to religion of any kind, so any conversation on the subject soon degenerated into argument. At Christmas and Easter he went to stay with his grandparents, who had nothing to do with the church. They weren't hostile to it, just indifferent.

So for Philip the strange little community provided by the Christian Union had been the only place where he could discuss his faith. There were some other independent individuals within it who were also beginning to ask the same kind of questions as himself, however, and they began to recommend books to each other and to discuss them. They persuaded the committee to invite a wider range of visiting speakers to the Christian Union, not just evangelicals but people representing other traditions within the church. One of these, Philip remembered, had recommended William James's lectures on *The Varieties of Religious Experience,* which he had found fascinating. While more conventional evangelicals proclaimed themselves 'born again', Philip started to refer to himself as 'twice-born' in James's sense, one who had been through 'the dark night of the soul', where all was hopeless, and emerged on the other side, with a positive vision of healing and redemption not to be mistaken for the primitive optimism of the 'once-born'.

This conscious assumption of superiority, of course, didn't do much for Philip's popularity among the rank and file of the Christian Union. Their mutterings about his 'intellectual arrogance' soon reached the attention of the Chairman, a quiet, reflective young man called Stephen, for whom Philip had great respect. The two of them had acted in a strange play, based on one of D.H.Lawrence's novels, about a family in Mexico to whom the old gods of the Aztecs had begun revealing themselves. Philip, whose voice at that time had still not broken, had been cast as Stephen's wife. He had had to practise walking in high heels for weeks, which had not gone unobserved in his boarding house. One consequence of this had been that whenever he walked past one group of sixth-formers they greeted him with wolf-whistles and kissing noises; another had been the friendship he had forged with Stephen, who had helped him through an otherwise embarrassing time.

Stephen, who wanted to come to Philip's aid again, took him aside one afternoon after school had finished and asked if they could speak for a while. The two wandered into one of the classrooms and sat down.

'This is Goo-Goo's room,' Philip announced. They called the bald young classics master Goo-Goo because he looked rather like an over-sized baby and spoke with a soft cooing sort of voice.

'That's not a very charitable nickname,' Stephen observed.

'Well, one can't be charitable all the time.'

'Perhaps not, though that's what our Lord asks of us.'

'Our Lord didn't have to sit through double lessons of Thucydides.'

'I'm afraid that's the kind of comment that people have been complaining about,' Stephen continued. 'They say that you're too clever sometimes for your own good. You should think more about the effect of your words on other people.'

'Other people should think more for themselves.'

'But our faith isn't just about thinking. It's about how we live and how we show our love for one another.'

'I suppose I do find it hard to take seriously what some of the others sometimes come out with,' Philip admitted. 'The other day one young third-year prayed for help with his Maths homework and I found it hard to take him seriously.'

'That's precisely it. You should show more sympathy. It matters to that boy that he does better in Maths. It's probably making him miserable, so it's not surprising that it should come up in his prayers.'

'Actually, I've been thinking about prayer recently,' Philip continued, 'especially petitionary prayer. Does God really want us to bombard him with prayers for all sorts of trivial things? And does He change His mind as a result? When you think about it, billions of people all over the world praying away, it doesn't make much sense.'

'There are quite a lot of things that don't make sense to us,' Stephen acknowledged. 'But we don't have to understand them completely. Don't worry so much about everything.'

That was exactly what his housemaster had told him the other day, when Philip had complained about compulsory chapel. He had actually been quite angry, partly because he had said at assembly that if anything was worrying them, they could come and talk to him, and Philip had called his bluff. It was one thing to have little atheists complaining about having to go to church on a Sunday but now he was getting it from earnest believers. Anyway, he had given young Philip a piece of his mind and told him that if he made such a fuss about something as small as this he would be grey before he was thirty.

Stephen was more patient with Philip, whom he genuinely liked. He told him to think more of others, whose faith might be disturbed by some of the questions he asked. Not that questioning wasn't necessary for development but there were ways of doing it which were less damaging to others. Philip, who found it easier to accept criticism from Stephen than from others, agreed to be more careful in future about what he said. But he felt reassured by the older boy's genuine concern and returned to his boarding house in a much happier frame of mind.

That night, after finishing his homework, Philip stood by the window of his cubicle (a narrow little space with just enough room for a bed, a chest of drawers and a desk, separated from the other cubicles by thin wooden partitions), looking out at the view across the playing fields to the railway line in the distance. On the far side of the railway line he could see the street lights and beyond that a cluster of houses. It wasn't the most glorious of views but for some reason it resonated deeply with him. Each of the houses, he reflected, contained people like himself trying to make sense of their time on earth. A train sped by on its way from London to the south coast. This too would be full of people on their own particular journeys. All of them were part of an astonishing and mysterious creation, which he would never fully understand. He remembered kneeling for a long time in silent wonder, feeling a tremendous sense of peace. Whether it was *Peace with God*, in Billy Graham's terms, he couldn't tell. Who was he, after all, to claim knowledge of God? But it was definitely peace, above and beyond the anxieties of his own life.

Chapter 2

Gospel

The whole tendency of the late 1960s, Philip recalled, had been towards the questioning of established ideas, whether in religion or politics. 1968, of course, had been the year of student protest throughout Europe. There had been barricades in the streets of Paris while in London there were demonstrations against the Vietnam War. Philip himself had been caught up in the excitement, he and his fellow sixth-formers demanding a Council of their own in which to discuss school policy. It was only advisory but the headmaster had to make at least a pretence of taking their suggestions seriously. Philip had played a prominent part in the debates, liking the sound of his own voice as much in the Council as on matters of faith.

1968 also stood out in his memory as the year in which he had met his first proper 'girlfriend'. He had been given permission that spring to attend a special weekend Sixth Form Conference on St.Matthew's Gospel on the grounds that it would help with his Religious Studies 'A' Level. He recalled the enthusiasm with which he had made his way to the station, the rucksack on his back containing not just his overnight clothes but two of his prize possessions: a parallel text of the New Testament in Greek and English and another recent acquisition, a commentary on St.Matthew's Gospel. This was part of a new series, the Pelican New Testament Commentaries, designed to bring the benefits of recent biblical criticism to a wider audience, to bridge the gap between academic research and the communities of faith.

Philip had initially been quite surprised to read on the opening page of the introduction to this commentary that one shouldn't approach the gospels 'expecting to find an accurate historical account of the life of Jesus'. He had thought that was what they purported to be. He soon grasped the idea, however, familiar from his classical studies, that ancient history was rather different from modern history. Those boring afternoons ploughing through Thucydides had at least taught him that ancient writers did not hesitate to put plausible speeches into the mouths of their protagonists with no evidence for doing so other than the fact that this was the sort of thing they might have been expected to say. And St.Matthew, as Philip discovered, seemed to have rather more evidence for the speeches he gave to Jesus than the Greek historian. There was not only St.Mark's Gospel but another common source that he shared with Luke (called Q) and a possible source of his own (called M). These were all collections of the teaching of Jesus as preserved by his first followers.

Philip had been so intent on what he had learnt about the gospels from his commentary that he almost missed his train, having to run the last part of the way to the station. He rushed up the stairs to the platform, wrenched open the carriage door and leapt in just as the train was beginning to move. He sank down on the nearest chair with a sense of relief, much to the amusement of two girls sitting opposite. One of them, a rather chubby girl, with a mass of frizzy hair and a cheerful face, giggled at his discomposure. Her companion, who was much prettier, with a clear, pale complexion and long black hair, smiled at him more sympathetically. It was a perennial dream of his that he would find himself on a train opposite a beautiful girl so he returned her smile with interest, explaining that he had been so lost in his thoughts that he had almost missed the train.

'A penny for them,' said the chubby girl. 'Your thoughts, I mean.'

'Oh, you wouldn't want to know.'

'Try us,' said the other girl, the pretty one.

Philip began to tell them about the conference on St.Matthew's Gospel only to discover that the girls too were attending it. They all laughed at the coincidence (not that unlikely given that the train was going to Folkestone, where the conference was being held) and introduced themselves. The pretty girl was called Faith and the chubby one Michelle; they went to a comprehensive in Barking and were, like Philip, taking Religious Studies as one of their 'A' levels. Philip recalled with some embarrassment that he was a little put off by their Essex twang although he too had spoken with a distinct South London accent at primary school before it had been drummed out of him. Unconsciously, as if in mimicry, his own accent began to creep back. He was attempting to explain the structure of St.Matthew's Gospel as described in his commentary, the way it arranged Jesus's teaching in five blocks of sayings, separated by accounts of miracles and other displays of power. These collections of sayings, including the Sermon on the Mount, shouldn't be thought of as actually spoken by Jesus in one go in a particular place. Matthew placed him on a mountain to reinforce the idea that he was a second Moses, teaching a new Law.

'When you come to think of it,' he concluded, 'you can't imagine someone sitting in the crowd, taking notes as Jesus spoke.'

'So how do we know that Jesus said any of these things?' asked Michelle.

'We don't, at least not for certain. But the sayings are probably authentic, as recalled by early disciples. The teaching itself is pretty amazing, so there's an argument for "self-authenticating genius" about it.'

'Self-whatting what?'

'Self-authenticating genius,' Philip repeated. 'The material is so strikingly original that it must have taken someone very special to produce it.'

'Like the Son of God,' Faith interrupted.

'Whatever that actually means. Jesus himself seems to have preferred the title Son of Man, which he took from apocalyptic writers like Daniel.' Philip hadn't actually read the Book of Daniel but they weren't to know that.

'Apo-cal-ypt-ic,' Michelle repeated slowly, playing dumber than she was.

'Yes, it means revelation, literally "unveiling" in Greek.'

The girls groaned in chorus, finally alerting Philip to the fact that he was irritating them with this parade of learning. He tried to introduce other topics of conversation, pretending an interest in pop songs, some of which he had actually heard because other boys in his corridor in the boarding house played their transistors so loud. Meanwhile he kept waiting for Faith to smile, which she did beautifully, but not nearly enough for his liking.

Faith, Philip recalled, seemed uncertain what to make of him. She had at first appeared to like him but may have been put off by his posh public school voice. He tried to explain that his school wasn't a traditional public school but Direct Grant, which meant that most of the boys were funded by the Inner London Education Authority. They had mostly, like himself, been to primary schools and were keen on football rather than rugby. He gained some street credibility with them by knowing some of the West Ham players but lost it soon after by having to admit that he had never heard of Alf Garnett.

'Gordon Bennett,' Michelle exclaimed. 'Not know our Alf!'

'We don't get to watch television at school,' Philip explained. 'And my parents don't even have a set.' They had recently returned from the Far East to Aldershot, a rather less exotic place to visit but easier to reach.

'So what do you do in the evenings?'

'Read, listen to music, talk.' Philip felt as if he needed to apologise for such middle-class habits.

They lapsed for a moment into silence, absorbing the differences between the lives they led. By now the train had passed through Sevenoaks and the suburbs of South London had given way to the open fields of Kent. They could see lambs, still unfamiliar with the noise of the train, running to their mothers for protection. Both Faith and Michelle oohed and aahed over the lambs, which lightened the atmosphere.

'So what do you want to be when you grow up?' Michelle asked, a fairly heavy dose of irony in her voice.

'I don't know. Some kind of teacher, I suppose.' Philip hadn't actually thought much about the future. He assumed that he would go to university and that some career path might become clearer after that. 'What about you?'

'I don't want to grow up,' Michelle began.

'A nurse,' Faith said. 'I've already applied to train, not far from you, actually. In Brixton.'

Brixton for Philip was a no-go area, a black ghetto which they were told at school not to visit. He'd only ever seen glimpses of it from the train travelling to Victoria.

'Not a place I'd have chosen to live,' he said.

'Someone's got to,' she replied. 'And it's cheap. We can't all go to university.'

'No, I suppose we can't.' Philip didn't actually know anyone in the upper sixth at school who had not applied to university but that merely showed what a hothouse his school was. The train meanwhile was picking up speed, rushing past hop fields and oasthouses, speeding through picturesque villages.

They decided to share a taxi from Folkestone Central and arrived in good time at the college where the conference was taking place. Official proceedings were due to begin at eleven with a lecture on 'Matthew and Mark'. There was time before that to register, collect their keys and find their rooms. The boys, Philip noted with disappointment, were separated from the girls by some distance. It was the story of his life. After familiarising himself with the rest of the campus, he made his way to the main lecture hall, where Faith and Michelle had already found places near the back. Faith's smile emboldened him to join them. She couldn't dislike him that much, Philip thought, resolving not to say anything too clever as he settled next to her. He wished now that he hadn't brought his parallel text of the New Testament. The hall meanwhile was filling up with healthy-looking, wholesome adolescents. He could feel Faith's shoulder against his own, noting with pleasure that she made no attempt to move away from him. Her blouse, he noticed, was a pale silky cream, matching her complexion. He had to make a real effort to bring his mind back to the subject of the gospels.

The lecture, however, delivered by a young bearded academic from King's College London, soon captured his interest. It focussed on some of the main differences between Mark, the earliest of the gospels, and Matthew,

33

who clearly based his narrative upon Mark, recounting many of the same events in the same basic order but from a somewhat different perspective. Mark's Jesus was apocalyptic (Philip couldn't help shooting a quick glance at Michelle at this point) expecting the imminent end of the world. It began with Jesus's baptism, after which he was portrayed calling on people to repent 'for the kingdom of God was at hand'. Matthew was more concerned to show that Jesus was the Messiah, hence its opening with that long genealogy tracing his descent back to Abraham. Hence too the infancy narrative, clearly constructed to show the fulfilment of Old Testament prophecies. Matthew's Jesus aimed to build a church community, commissioning the disciples at the end to preach to the whole world. Mark, in contrast, presented the disciples as stupid, forever failing to understand Jesus. In Matthew the more obscure parables were explained to them as 'insiders', unlike the Scribes and Pharisees, who remained obstinately 'outside' the kingdom.

What this revealed, according to the speaker, was the original context and purpose of Matthew's gospel, which was written after the expulsion of Christians from the synagogues around 85 AD. Those who refused to recognise Jesus as the Christ, the Messiah predicted by the prophets, had quickly come to be seen as enemies of the early Church. Hence their hostile portrait in Matthew's gospel, where they not only asked difficult questions in an attempt to trap him but succeeded finally in bringing about his death. Most shocking of all was the imprecation the Jews were made to visit upon themselves in calling for his death: 'His blood be upon us, and upon our children.' Matthew's hostility towards 'the Jews', the lecturer observed, could be said to have fed nearly two millennia of Christian anti-semitism.

There was more detailed material in the lecture, showing how Matthew's additions to Mark were either based on different sources, some of which he shared with Luke, or assembled from Old Testament citations, for instance in the temptation in the wilderness, where it was not only Satan who quoted from the Book of Deuteronomy but Jesus himself, all of his replies coming from that source. Even the famous cry of dereliction on the cross, 'My God, my God, why hast thou forsaken me?', could be traced to the opening verse of Psalm 22. It seemed hard to believe that Christ would have indulged in quotation at this grim moment; more probably, Matthew composed the scene with reference to the scriptures as part of his ongoing attempt to portray Jesus as fulfilling them.

There was some time for questions at the end of the lecture, most of them from earnest evangelicals unable to accept that each detail of the gospel wasn't literally true. The lecturer, however, challenged them to consider some of the more 'poetic' elements in the gospel. The angels involved in the infancy and resurrection narratives, for example, were part of a different world picture to our own; they weren't really integral to the story, at least to the way in which we would now tell it. Even the miraculous 'virgin-birth' rested to some extent on a mistranslation from the original Hebrew in Isaiah 7:14 (which referred to a young woman giving birth) to the Greek of the Septuagint (where she became a virgin). At this point it was the turn of the Catholics in the audience to feel uneasy. The mood in the hall as they traipsed out for lunch was decidedly more sombre than when they entered.

'I don't know about you,' Michelle began, 'but I was always taught to read Matthew as gospel.'

'Yes, I don't see where the good news is in an anti-semitic diatribe,' Faith agreed.

'It's not a diatribe,' Philip countered. 'It's just that Matthew was writing when those Jews who didn't accept Jesus as the Messiah were regarded by Christians as religious opponents. Jesus himself had challenged the Temple authorities. You had to choose sides; either you were for him or against.'

'Well, it sounded as if Christians were responsible for the holocaust,' Faith complained.

'Some of them were,' Philip replied. 'They could certainly have done more to prevent it.'

'Soup or salad?' interposed Michelle, attempting to lighten the mood. 'You have to choose.'

They moved through the cafeteria, making their selection, and sat with a group of people Michelle knew from an earlier conference. Philip was introduced as going to a posh school where they studied Greek and never watched telly, which kept him quiet for most of the time. Checking his programme, he noted that he was in the same seminar group as Faith for the afternoon session, when they were going to discuss Matthew chapter 5. He would have to keep quiet about having learnt it by heart in the first form. He was beginning to wonder whether his attraction to her was simply a matter of hormones. What kind of relationship could they have if he were forced perpetually to hide his true thoughts and feelings? He noticed that she was distinctly cooler towards him than she had been earlier. He made his apologies and left for a breath of fresh air before the afternoon sessions began.

The seminar itself was largely uneventful. There had been some initial discussion of translation when it emerged that some were using the Authorised Version, some the Revised and others the New English Bible, which translated verse 3, 'How blest are those that know that they are poor.' Most of the other translations said 'poor in spirit', which Philip argued was clearer and closer to the original Greek. 'You can't help knowing that you are poor,' he added, glancing at Faith to see if she was impressed or angry. It was hard to tell. The discussion mainly focussed on the way Jesus was made to contrast his teaching with that of the old Law, making it clear that he expected his followers not only not to kill but not even to be angry, not only not to commit adultery but not even to look at a woman 'lustfully'. Philip kept his own eyes firmly on the page. It seemed a bit harsh of Jesus to expect him to pluck out his eye or to cut off his right hand rather than go to hell. He considered asking if these were references to voyeurism and masturbation respectively but he was not prepared to risk offending Faith even more.

After the seminar Philip went for a walk along the Leas, the cliff-top gardens overlooking the beach. He wandered fairly aimlessly along the cliff-top path past seemingly endless hotels, outside which were benches full of elderly people enjoying the late afternoon sunshine. Down below, facing the pebble beach below the cliff, there was a kind of fairground, with dodgems and other rides, which looked fairly dilapidated. Further along were some beach huts, which also looked pretty run down. A sprinkling of people in deckchairs sat in front of the huts eating ice-cream or candy floss. He was returning towards the college, not really noticing where he was going, when he stumbled across Faith and Michelle eating ice-cream on a bench.

'The wanderer returns,' Michelle observed. 'Don't worry so much, it might never happen.'

'Whatever *it* is,' Faith added, granting another of her beatific smiles. All was not lost, then, Philip thought, joining them on the bench.

'I can't say I'm that impressed with Folkestone,' he opined.

'Not up to your standards?' teased Michelle.

Philip gave what was supposed to be a Gallic shrug, as if to say that he surrendered, guilty as charged. They talked about their respective schools and teachers, Philip recounting some fairly embarrassing episodes of sexual harassment from members of staff. The girls were both indignant; at least their teachers tended to flirt with pupils of the opposite sex. They made their way slowly back to the college in time for the evening meal, after which they filtered back into the lecture room for a showing of Pasolini's recent film, *The Gospel According to St.Matthew*.

Philip was disappointed with the movie, as he told the girls afterwards. It was almost too reverent, too respectful of tradition, retaining all the miraculous elements, including the angel appearing to Joseph at the beginning.

'You don't expect a gay Gramscian Marxist to believe in angels,' he said.

'I didn't know he was gay,' Michelle said. 'And Gramscian, whatever that is, sounds even worse. I certainly didn't like his portrait of Jesus, who seemed angry all the time.'

'Well, he's portrayed like that in the gospel too,' Philip countered.

'Not all the time,' said Faith.

'Maybe not,' Philip admitted. 'But he is shown to be quite moody, for instance when he curses the fig tree. And he shouts at the Pharisees a lot.'

'You brood of vipers!' mimicked Michelle. 'I thought the best bits were those in which Jesus wasn't involved, the scene of Salome dancing for Herod, for example, and Judas throwing back the thirty pieces of silver and hanging himself. That was great!'

'Nothing like a good hanging,' Philip agreed. 'Did you know that Pasolini got his mother to play Mary?

38

Not the pregnant young Mary at the beginning, of course, but the older Mary at the foot of the cross.'

By now they were wandering back towards their rooms and the girls invited Philip back for a coffee. He tried not to look too pleased but he felt really mature, as if he were already at university. It was pathetic really, he told himself, that he had never been asked into a girl's room in his life before this. Not that this counted as a romantic assignation; they spent most of the time discussing matters of faith. Philip told them about the commitment he had made at the Billy Graham crusade only to discover that Faith and her parents had sung in the choir there.

'Well, you were very good,' Philip said. 'Probably the best thing about the evening.'

'Didn't you like Billy Graham himself?' she asked.

'I was quite impressed at the time. But when I thought about it afterwards, I felt he was a bit heavy on sin and evil. Still, it did the trick.'

'It's not a trick,' Faith objected. 'I've never encountered anyone so straightforward and sincere.'

'Oh, he's sincere. I don't doubt that. But his message is a bit too black and white.'

'But don't you have to choose between good and evil, light and dark?'

'And if you make the wrong choice,' interrupted Michelle in the closest she could muster to a Southern drawl, 'you will be doomed to hell!'

'Yes, that's precisely it,' Philip continued. 'He tries to scare people into faith by threatening them with eternal damnation.'

'But doesn't Jesus talk about hell?' asked Faith.

'He certainly talks about weeping and gnashing of teeth but they could all refer to inner torments, a state of mind rather than a literal place. *Gehenna*, of course, was a place where they burnt rubbish outside the city of

Jerusalem.'

'Trust you to know that,' complained Michelle.

They went on to discuss the difficulties of reading the Bible. At first Faith insisted that she found no difficulty in reading the gospels but when Philip questioned her closely about the infancy narratives in Matthew and Luke, she had to admit that there were aspects of the Christmas story that it was hard to take literally. But then what became of all those lovely carols about sheep and donkeys, camels and wise men?

'You can still sing them,' Philip argued 'as long as you don't take them too literally.'

'Oh thanks. We have your permission to sing carols so long as we don't take them seriously.'

The discussion continued, with Michelle acting as referee. She could see that there was something between Philip and Faith, a spark of attraction which added zest to the debate. They were both from sheltered backgrounds, Faith by virtue of her strict evangelical parents and Philip as a result of his schooling. But they were both seventeen and could not entirely ignore the youthful blood beating through their veins. Philip would wonder later how many other young couples had conducted their courtship mainly through the language of theology. Increasingly few, he decided. But it was the language which mattered most to them and which they shared. It was not until the early hours of the morning that Philip returned to his room.

At breakfast the following morning they kept to matters of marmalade and fruit juice. Philip had bought a paper and was mulling over the football scores. West Ham had won again, he noted, with goals from Hurst and Peters, news which left the girls unimpressed. The conference resumed with another lecture, this time on Matthew's account of the Passion and Resurrection. Philip listened intently, making detailed notes on all the

Old Testament references. There were small group discussions afterwards, followed by lunch, which marked the end of the conference. The girls agreed to take the same train as Philip up to London and during the journey he plucked up courage to ask Faith if they could meet again, maybe to see a film. She agreed rather reluctantly to give Philip her home telephone number.

'Nothing too highbrow,' she insisted. 'I couldn't take another Pasolini film.'

'I don't think I could either,' Philip admitted. But he got out at Bromley South feeling very pleased with life. It would be his first ever date. He spent the next few weeks dreaming of Faith, both awake and asleep. He couldn't quite decide what it was that he liked best about her; was it her hair, her mouth, her complexion, her figure? Certainly not her mind, but that could be worked on. He already cast himself as a young Professor Higgins bring his fair lady from East London up to his own exalted level. She was as pretty as Audrey Hepburn, he thought, and could sing as well.

They met a few times that summer, normally on a Saturday, when they were both free. They would meet at Victoria Station and then make their way to whichever cinema or theatre they had chosen. They disagreed sometimes over their choice of film, Philip insisting, for instance, that they go to Polanski's new film, *Rosemary's Baby*, which she found disturbing and distasteful. Sometimes they went to concerts, which taxed his rather limited knowledge of music. They normally went for a meal afterwards, nothing very upmarket, a Pizza place or a Joe Lyons. Gradually they got used to each other, learning more about each other's very different worlds.

Physically their relationship was very limited. They kissed on meeting and parting and held hands in the

41

cinema. Faith also allowed him occasionally allowed him to put his arm around her if it was really dark. Anything more than that was strictly off limits. In retrospect, Philip found it hard to believe that this had all taken place in the supposedly 'swinging sixties'. Elsewhere in London the girls were wearing short skirts, experimenting with drugs and sleeping around (so people said). But for Philip and Faith it had been very different. Philip thought about inviting her to stay with his parents but she would have been shocked by their hostility to anything religious, not to mention how much they drank. They in turn would have considered her priggish and frigid. He was beginning to think that himself, especially when she refused to see *Hair* because of its notorious nudity. But their Saturday meetings remained the highlight of his otherwise rather dull week.

Chapter 3

Creed

Philip continued seeing Faith regularly during his final term at school, while he was cramming for the Oxford scholarship exams and she was a student nurse in Brixton. They used to meet sometimes in Brixton itself (Philip overcoming his fear of the area), sometimes at school (where Faith came to the occasional play or concert) and sometimes, as before, in central London. They were still somewhere between lovers and friends. Philip certainly felt 'in love' with Faith but she still refused to allow him any sexual license, which became a source of increasing tension between them.

'The other nurses let their boyfriends stay for the night,' he complained one evening, as they sat over coffee in her bedroom in the nurses' accommodation block. The fact that her narrow room was dominated by the bed made his frustration all the more intense.

'Not all of them. Anyway, you'll just have to wait,' Faith insisted. 'I don't think either of us is ready.'

'You know you're placing me in danger. I might have to cut my right hand off rather than be sent to hell.'

It was a perennial argument whenever he visited her. On other occasions the opportunity and therefore the subject didn't arise. Faith was genuinely uncertain of the future. She wasn't enjoying nursing and had applied to university for the following year. Philip was planning to work for a charity in Africa for six months from January and she wasn't sure that their relationship was strong enough to survive a prolonged break of this kind. She came to see him onto the plane to Nairobi, however, very much approving of his decision to give at least a short period of his life to helping others.

Philip looked back at his time in Kenya with mixed feelings. It had been good for him, taking him out of his narrow academic world; he had also been able to do some good for the children he taught there. But in some respects it was an equally narrow world within which he worked in Nairobi. He saw little of the rest of Africa, the charity for which he worked being careful to protect him from danger. He was taken to see some of the outlying villages, gaining at least some awareness of the primitive conditions in which people had to live there. He returned eager to get started on his English degree. He had won a scholarship to Oxford while Faith had been given a place at Lancaster University to read Religious Studies.

Oxford turned out (for him at least) to be merely an extension of school. He was at an all-male college, where he ate all his meals. His closest friends came from his college (and were therefore male). He met other men through sport. He had been told that lectures were a good place to pick up girls but his own attempts to do so were firmly rebuffed. There were girls in the choir he joined but his initial attempt at asking one of them out was spectacularly unsuccessful. One of the altos seemed more interested, sending him an invitation to attend an audition for a play at her college, which puzzled him.

'I didn't even know they were doing a play,' he said to one of the other tenors.

'They probably aren't,' came the reply. 'It's just a way of making contact.'

Philip thought she must be fairly desperate to resort to something like that but turned up nevertheless for his 'audition' only to discover, as his friend had suspected, that there was no-one there but the rather giggly alto. He agreed to go to a performance of the St.Matthew Passion with her but the whole event was something of a fiasco. She lamented the fact that Bach had been restricted to sacred subjects, than which he, of course, could see nothing more important. It became increasingly obvious that they had absolutely nothing in common. He tried going to the occasional Saturday night disco but these proved to be too much like cattle markets for his puritanical taste. There would be groups of males propping up the bar while clusters of females girated to the music as attractively as they could, waiting for a tap on the shoulder. Philip decided that it would be better to wait until he met someone 'naturally'.

Faith's experiences at Lancaster, as Philip discovered when they met in London at the end of the first term, were disappointing for different reasons. The accommodation was mixed there, men and women living in the same halls of residence, though on different floors. Since the campus was a couple of miles from the city of Lancaster itself, they spent most of their time there. There were similar discos at which couples paired off, the only difference being that their rooms were conveniently to hand. Faith found it hard to work surrounded by the unmistakable noises of enthusiastic lovemaking and blaring music. She resorted to the library as much as possible as a haven of peace and quiet amid the Sodom and Gomorrah in which she had landed.

Philip couldn't help laughing at her account of the campus, which he was certain must be exaggerated. He was also pleased that Faith felt that she could confide in him, as a friend if nothing more. They arranged to share a cottage in the Lake District for a week that Easter; she would invite a friend from Lancaster and he one from

Oxford to make a party of four. They found a suitable place not far from Keswick and the following April Philip and his friend Aidan joined Faith and her friend Anne in Lancaster in preparation for their week together. Aidan was a theology student, a Roman Catholic who attended some of the Anglican services in Philip's college in the ecumenical spirit encouraged by the Second Vatican Council. He had explained for Philip's benefit the significance not only of that council but of some of the earlier councils in the history of the Church, at which key Christian doctrines had been settled. Philip had quickly found that he learnt more from conversations with Aidan and other students than from his actual tutorials. He was a little concerned, however, at the reaction he might provoke in Faith, who had been taught to be very suspicious of Rome. Aidan in turn seemed less than comfortable with the girls, at least on their first meeting.

That initial encounter with Faith and Anne in a pub in Lancaster didn't augur at all well for the coming week. Anne was clearly nervous, giggling uncomfortably and blushing, which made Aidan treat her as if she were a rather badly-behaved child.

'How did you two meet?' Philip asked the two girls, trying to break the ice a little.

'In the library,' Faith replied.

'Ah, refugees from Sodom.' Anne looked baffled by this so Philip explained that he had heard of the goings-on in the halls of residence.

'We discovered that we were doing some of the same courses,' Faith continued, 'studying the same texts. So we used to have coffee together and discuss them.'

'Then one thing led to another,' Philip mocked. He had briefly developed a theory that Faith was a closet lesbian, hence her resistance to his charms. He found the idea curiously exciting if highly unlikely. 'I suppose you two will want to share a room in the cottage.'

'Well, it would make sense,' Faith agreed. There were only two bedrooms, one with a double bed, the other with two singles.

'We could draw lots over who sleeps where,' Aidan suggested. 'There are precedents in the early church.'

Philip explained that Aidan had been following a course of lectures on the early centuries of the Church. He now regarded himself as an expert on heresy, especially on the Gnostics.

'Who are the Gnostics when they are at home?' Anne asked. 'Sounds like a band.'

Aidan told them about the discoveries at Nag Hammadi on the Upper Nile just after the end of the war, including papyri of a number of Gnostic Gospels which had recently been translated into English. They had transformed our understanding of early Christianity, he claimed.

'There's some amazing material in them. There's one, for example, *The Gospel of Philip*, in which Jesus is presented as kissing Mary Magdalen on the lips.' This brought cries of disbelief from the two girls.

'Well, there's actually a lacuna at that point,' Aidan continued, 'a hole in the papyrus. He could have kissed her somewhere else but most scholars assume it was there. The other disciples go on to ask why he loves her more than them. So the suggestion is that there was something between them, according to Philip at least. Some of the Gnostics were quite libertarian about sexual matters. They didn't think the material world mattered very much, which sometimes made them ascetic (denying the flesh) but sometimes turned them in the other direction (denying the importance of whatever they did in the flesh). Clement refers to a *Secret Gospel of St.Mark* in which the young man in

47

the linen cloth who flees naked from the Garden of Gethsemane is reported to have spent the night with Jesus in a cave.'

'Gordon Bennett!' Faith exclaimed. 'No wonder they were suppressed. How many of these alternative gospels are there?'

'Quite a few,' Aidan continued. 'Not all of them have survived, of course, which makes the discoveries at Nag Hammadi so exciting. We knew of their existence because of references to them in the Church Fathers, but could only guess at their contents on the basis of their brief and normally disapproving citations from them. Now we have a clearer picture, one that may grow as more manuscripts are discovered, like the Dead Sea Scrolls. Who knows what else may emerge from the deserts of the Middle East?'

'How come most people don't know about these other gospels?' Anne asked.

'Most people don't know much about anything. And the Church has always controlled what the faithful are told, my Church at least, once Christianity became the official religion of the Roman Empire. Before that there was more debate about what being a Christian entailed.'

'I'm seriously thinking of becoming a Gnostic,' Anne ventured.

'It wasn't always that much fun,' Aidan explained. 'You had to abandon interest in the material world as the work of the Demiurge. They were dualists, making a huge division between the world of the spirit and that of the flesh.'

'Like Faith,' muttered Philip bitterly.

'I've heard all about you and your interest in the flesh,' Anne commented.

'From a very doubtful source.'

'Oh no, a very reliable one. I trust her implicitly. It's

you I don't trust. I'll be keeping a wary eye on you in the cottage.'

At this point the four of them moved away from the early centuries of the Church to discuss more mundane topics such as food for the coming week. Faith suggested that they stock up at the supermarket next to the bus station in Keswick. From there it was a fairly short journey to their cottage in Braithwaite.

It turned out to be a fairly wet week. They spent the first day trudging around Keswick in the rain with all the other frustrated walkers in anoraks and boots, treating themselves to cream teas and second-hand books. After that they decided simply to ignore the weather. Their first outing took in the stone circle at Castlerigg, which prompted a lecture from Aidan on sacrifice in the ancient world. They then took the path up to Walla Crag and were rewarded with a magnificent view of Derwent Water and its surrounding hills. They resolved to do Cat Bells, which they could see on the far side of the lake, the following day and Skiddaw, looming above them to the right, the day after that.

'Ah yes, the principle of development,' announced Aidan. 'We gradually build up our strength and our faith.' He started to outline Newman's famous essay on the subject, which he had written while agonising over whether or not to join the Catholic Church. In order to convert, Aidan explained, he needed a theory to account for the gradual development of doctrines such as those concerning Our Lady, for which there was little support in scripture. Faith pricked up her ears at this, since devotion to Mary (or Mariolatry, as she had been taught to call it) had always puzzled her.

'The point,' Aidan continued, 'is that the official teaching of the Church always lags behind the practice of the faithful. It took centuries, for example, for the

Church to work out the ramifications of belief in the incarnation, how to understand the term "Son of God".'

'It seems pretty straightforward to me,' Anne protested.

'That's because you're so used to saying it every week. Even you must struggle with the next phrase in the Nicene Creed, "eternally begotten of the Father", especially when it goes on, "begotten, not made".'

'Yes, what's that all about?' Faith asked, surprised to find herself genuinely interested.

'It's about establishing Jesus not as a "creature" made by God but part of God's own essence. The debates were quite acrimonious before both extremes were eventually ruled to be heretical. If you argued that Jesus had one nature, the divine, you were a Monophysite. If you went to the other extreme, and argued that he was merely a human being, you were Arian or Apollinarian, heresies named after the theologians who advocated that position. In the end, it was resolved at the Council of Chalcedon, which ruled that Christ was both fully human and fully divine.'

'Isn't that a bit of a fudge? ' Anne objected.

'Or a paradox,' Aidan resumed. 'Whatever you want to call it, it defined the limits of orthodox Christian teaching. If you denied either aspect of Christ, his humanity or his divinity, you weren't part of the Church.'

'We're not part of your Church anyway,' Anne pointed out.

'Well, that was what worried Newman,' Aidan continued, undeterred by the personal animosity that was creeping into Anne's voice. 'He came to the conclusion that Anglicans were heretics, no longer in communion with the one true Church. But before he could become a Catholic, he had to convince himself that there was sufficient justification for some of the later developments in doctrine, for instance those relating to Mary.'

'I have problems with those myself,' Philip admitted.

'I remember the lecturer at the conference on Matthew arguing that belief in the Virgin Birth developed from a mistranslation into Greek of the Hebrew for young girl,' Faith added.

'However it might have begun,' Aidan replied, 'it quickly became part of Christian orthodoxy. Mind you, one of my professors argues that much early Christian doctrine answers questions of the time which we don't really ask now. Having studied how Christian doctrine was first "made" he thinks we need to "remake" Christian doctrine in terms of modern thought.'

'Wouldn't that soon appear outdated?' Philip asked. 'By the time you had come up with one reworking of Christian faith, say in terms of existentialism, people would have moved on to something even more modern.'

'Precisely,' Aidan agreed. 'We're probably better off keeping to the traditional formulations, which have lasted for the best part of two thousand years. We can always interpret them historically, making allowances for the period in which they were formulated. That's what we do with other ancient texts.'

'Or we could just continue to believe them,' said Faith.

The girls had by now heard enough of Aidan's pontificating and suggested that it was time to return to the cottage. As they made their descent, Philip told Faith about some of the difficulties he had encountered with an evangelical group in his college. He had first annoyed them by asking what they deemed 'inappropriate' questions about biblical texts and then by questioning some of their other activities. They went once a week, for example, to visit a hospital on the outskirts of Oxford, talking to patients and then singing a few hymns for them. Visiting the sick was clearly one of the things Jesus expected of his followers, but Philip had become increasingly embarrassed by the crudity of some of the hymns they sang. This hadn't gone down at all well with the others, who accused him of elitism and snobbery, and in the end he just stopped going. He had then tried the college chapel only to discover that the chaplain was a rather camp Anglo-Catholic of an almost Brideshead vintage. He had recently started accompanying Aidan to Mass at Blackfriars but felt equally uncomfortable there too, unfamiliar with the ritual. So for the moment there was no place of worship in which he felt at home.

'Well, you were always difficult to please,' Faith commented, 'always the odd one out. You're like Groucho Marx, refusing to become a member of any club that would actually accept you.'

'It's easy for you. You were brought up in the faith. You were even christened Faith.'

'Don't think that makes it any easier. Anyway, you know next to nothing about my background.'

'That's true.'

'Partly because you never asked. You're always too busy talking about yourself.'

Philip recognised the truth in this too and apologised. So for the first time Faith told him about some of her own difficulties in being brought up as strictly as she had been by parents whose love for her she had never questioned but whose rules she had found hard to accept. She had had to fight hard, for example, to be allowed to meet Philip, who had only been found acceptable because he had been encountered at such an obviously 'religious' conference.

'I told them what a nice boy you were,' Faith explained. 'Little did they know.'

'It must be great to have complete freedom at Lancaster,' Philip acknowledged.

'Well, it's going from one extreme to the other. I was always fighting against the rules at home; now I'm fighting against the complete absence of rules on campus.'

'So have you found people with whom you can fit in?' Philip asked.

'A few individuals, I suppose, like Anne. And there's a church we go to in Lancaster, which we like. We have evening meetings at which we discuss the readings for that week over coffee and biscuits. Anne and I both go, partly just to get off campus and away from all the drinking.'

At this point Anne, who couldn't face Aidan telling her about one more early-church heresy, caught up with them.

'Are you talking about gorgeous George?' she asked, causing Faith blushingly to explain that he was the curate at this church in Lancaster.

'He's really handsome,' Anne continued rather mischievously. 'And I'm sure he fancies Faith.'

Philip saw that Faith was embarrassed and changed the subject. He had wondered, however, whether Faith had transferred her affections to someone else. Given how attractive she was, it had been surely a matter of time before someone else noticed her. He might have known that it would be a man of the cloth, a wolf in sheep's clothing. They walked the final part of the way back to their cottage in silence.

The rest of the week passed uneventfully. They had managed to reach the top of Skiddaw, though for the last few hundred yards they had been completely enveloped in cloud. They paid the obligatory visit to

Dove Cottage, where Philip treated them to a recital of "Tintern Abbey", which he had learnt by heart at school. They followed the path around the lake at Grasmere consuming large amounts of local gingerbread and committing Aidan to a vow of silence. It would be good practice, they suggested, for a possible career as a Trappist monk. Anne never left Faith's side, preventing Philip from interrogating her further about gorgeous George. So they reached the end of the week without the subject being raised.

Chapter 4

Oxford

Philip's suspicions about the Reverend George Wilcox proved not without foundation. 'Gorgeous George' did indeed have his eye on Faith. Soon he had more than his eye on her, being allowed, as Philip had been earlier, to put his arm around her when accompanying her to films. As a clergyman, of course, he couldn't show the same impatience as Philip at the slowness with which his courtship developed. Faith was five or six years younger than he was and technically she was in his charge as a young parishioner of whom he should not take advantage. Slowly but surely, however, their relationship progressed and it was no surprise to anyone when he asked her to marry him and she accepted. For he was not only gorgeous but generous, genuinely caring for what she thought, listening to her worries and doubts, constantly reassuring her and making her feel secure.

Philip's reaction when she told him this was to mimic being sick. But he had offered his congratulations, albeit through clenched teeth. George was a good man, he could see that; he could also recognise that he would probably make her happy. He and Aidan once more made the journey to Lancaster together to attend the wedding, which took place on a sunny summer's day in the church where Faith and George had first met.

'Yes,' Philip acknowledged to Anne as they were watching the photographs being taken after the service. 'Even I have to admit that they seem made for one another.'

'Is that supposed to be ironic?' Anne asked.

'No, I mean it. They are very well matched: a marriage made in heaven.'

'Just get over it,' came the reply.

And Philip found, somewhat to his own surprise, that he did. It helped that he was going to spend the rest of the summer in Florence, learning Italian for a special option he was taking in his final year at Oxford on the influence of Italian on English Literature in the sixteen century. A friend of his had taken this option the previous year and recommended it, not least because there were college grants available to fund a summer in Italy. So barely a week after Faith's wedding Philip found himself on the train from Munich to Florence, waking early in the morning to views of the foothills of the Alps. This, he told himself, was life. Who would want to settle down in marriage when there was so much of the world still to explore?

His first views of Florence itself were something of a disappointment. Expecting church domes and spires, grand renaissance palaces and galleries, what he actually saw were large blocks of modern flats already running to seed. The station itself, named after the nearby church of Santa Maria Novella, was more impressive but he had difficulty identifying the landlady with whom he was staying, who had arranged to meet him at the station. She had described herself, not very helpfully, as 'small and old, with grey hair' but the platform was positively swarming with little old ladies answering to that description. Eventually, however, most of them disappeared, leaving only one obvious candidate, who whisked him off to her house in the north of the city.

The language course for which he had enrolled took place in the Scuola Dante Alighieri, a rather grand villa on the far side of the river from the Uffizi. Philip noted at the initial welcome meeting that the other members of his class were a motley collection of ages and nationalities. He also noticed that there were some fairly stunning girls among them, one of whom, a dark girl with an athletic figure, came over to talk to him.

'So where are you from?' she asked.

'A good question,' he replied. 'My family have moved all over the place but I'm now studying at Oxford.'

'Impressive. I'm from Newcastle myself.' She pronounced it with the stress on the second syllable, saying the first syllable as if it were spelt 'niur', which didn't at first register with Philip.

'Where's that?' he asked in all innocence.

'On the Tyne, of course, where it's always been.'

'Sorry, I haven't studied Geordie. And I've never been that far north. What do you do there?'

'Music,' she replied. 'What about you?'

Philip went through his usual routine about the influence of Italian on English literature, watching her eyes glaze over as he did so. But they were beautiful eyes with large bluey-green irises. She was also beautifully tanned, positively glowing with youth and energy. He asked which particular composers she was studying.

'Well, Verdi's my main interest but I need to learn more about Italian opera in general.'

'A Geordie into Verdi,' he mused. 'It doesn't quite fit the stereotype.'

'Nor do I, pet,' she laughed. 'And by the way, my name's Rachel.'

He introduced himself to her and together they met some of the other pupils on the course before moving on to a nearby restaurant for lunch. Afterwards they joined the throng of tourists outside the Duomo, which

Rachel suggested that they explore together. Her evident interest in him was something of a new experience for him but he tried not to seem too surprised or too eager. He noticed that she dipped her fingers into the stoup of holy water at the entrance and crossed her forehead.

'So you're a Catholic?' he said.

'Yes, hun, but don't worry, I don't bite.' Philip hadn't ever been addressed as 'hun' before but found that he rather liked it. They strolled around the pleasantly cool interior of the Cathedral, adjusting to the dim light. Rachel, who had visited Florence before, explained that the baptistery had a more exciting décor, including frescos of the devil swallowing sinners.

'You can see their legs sticking out of his mouth,' she explained cheerfully, 'spouts of blood pouring from his teeth.'

Philip, not for the last time during his stay in Florence, found himself puzzling over the mixture of sophistication and naivety she displayed. Her response to art was always fresh and vivid, as if she were seeing things for the first time. It soon became evident, however, that she was very familiar with many of the paintings and was able to tell him a great deal about them. But she seemed to enjoy gelati as much as Botticelli. Italian ice-cream had come as a revelation to Philip as well but he couldn't get quite as excited about it as she did. There was a sensuality about her which simultaneously shocked and aroused him. She was also very direct. At the end of the first week of the course she invited him for a meal in her flat, which was both more comfortable and more stylishly furnished than his own modest room in the suburbs. It belonged, she explained, to one of her lecturers, who rented it to students at reasonable rates. She had prepared a pasta salad which they ate on the balcony overlooking the river, talking about their respective families and friends, both at school and university. Then she led him back into the living room, sitting beside him on the sofa.

'Did anyone ever tell you that you're cute?' she asked.

'Only my piano teacher as he slid his hand under my bum.'

'Funny, too, if a little repressed. Don't you like me?'

'Of course I do. It's just that I've never met anyone quite like you.'

'Well, you've obviously led a sheltered existence,' she said, giving him a soft kiss on the cheek.

'I thought you Catholics were supposed to be the inhibited ones.'

'It's all that repression that makes us so excitable. Having to confess all our secrets. We brood upon them endlessly.'

They advanced quickly from gentle kissing to more passionate embraces and she suggested that they might be more comfortable on the bed. Philip's initial reaction, he was embarrassed to recall, had been one of fear.

'But we hardly know each other,' he objected.

'All the more reason for getting to know each other better,' she countered. 'Don't worry, I'll be gentle with you. And yes, I am taking precautions.'

They slowly undressed each other and crept under the duvet. She certainly knew what she was doing, which was more than he did. It worried him briefly that she was clearly so experienced in the art of love but he was grateful that she made all the moves, taking the pressure off him. His main concern was that he would come too soon. He tried desperately to think of the most boring topics imaginable, Anglo-Saxon grammar, the stanza formation of the Italian sonnet, Wordsworth's Odes, but all to no avail. Years of youthful frustration could not be stemmed, flooding out in a torrent of relief. He stammered an apology.

'No need,' she said, 'no need. You must have kept that bottled up for a long time. And anyway, you weren't bad for a beginner. You'll get better with practice, as your piano teacher might have said.'

This sounded like a well-rehearsed line but Philip accepted the reassurance gratefully. And her prediction was true. He quickly overcame his inhibitions as they spent almost every afternoon in her flat.

'So that's why the Italians have a siesta,' he laughed after one particularly long afternoon in her bed.

'Yes, pet, and that's why the English come to Italy to learn how to live.'

Philip managed to stifle a reference to E.M.Forster but not the accompanying reminder that he would have to return to Oxford in a few weeks. He had allowed himself for the first time in his life to live in the moment but that moment was about to pass. He began to turn his mind towards ways in which he and Rachel could perhaps stay together, possibly in Oxford. It had always been his intention to stay there as a postgraduate and there was a professor in the Music department who specialised in Verdi, on whom she had said she was keen to do more research. He mentioned the possibility to her and was relieved to discover that she took up the idea enthusiastically.

'We'll do well to get grants, mind,' she said.

'Well, it would give us an incentive in our final year.'

This proved to be the case. Like many other students before and since, Rachel and Philip buckled down to their work in the final year of their degree. They allowed themselves the occasional break; Rachel enjoyed exploring Oxford and Philip discovered an enthusiasm for the North-east which surprised some of his southern friends.

'You should see the beach at Bamburgh, beyond the castle,' he told Aidan. 'It stretches for miles.'

'Don't pretend it's the beaches you go for,' Aidan replied rather sniffily.

'Well, maybe not. But they are beautiful.'

'And so is Rachel.'

Aidan had been unable to resist making jokes about the number of years for which Jacob had had to work to win the biblical Rachel's hand. He didn't altogether approve of Philip's belated entry into the 1960s. But he could see that Philip was serious about the relationship and welcomed his renewed interest in Catholicism, whatever its underlying motive. Rachel too surprised her friends by the seriousness with which she was now treating her studies. She heard at the end of June that she had succeeded in getting a first but Philip had to wait nervously until after his viva in August to discover that he too had been successful. Both were awarded grants and wasted no time in finding somewhere to live, a small house in a terrace in East Oxford, just off the Cowley Road. He and Rachel shared the master bedroom at the front of the house, leaving the two small bedrooms to Aidan and a friend of his from the divinity faculty.

It was useful for Philip to be sharing the house with two theology students since his research involved religious novels of the mid-nineteenth century, when the increasingly popular genre had become a battleground for competing theological positions. He became especially interested in a group of historical novels published in the 1850s, set in motion by Charles Kingsley's *Hypatia,* a barely disguised attack on Roman Catholicism and its supposed fear of the flesh.

Set in fifth-century Alexandria, it portrayed bands of ravening monks roaming the streets of that ancient seat of learning. It reached a violent climax with the monks tearing the eponymous heroine, a beautiful neo-platonist teacher, limb from limb. To such ends, Kingsley implied, does asceticism lead. Cardinal Nicholas Wiseman, newly appointed Archbishop of Westminster, decided to retaliate with a series of novels representing Catholicism in a more favourable light. His own contribution, *Fabiola*, celebrated the conversion of its eponymous heroine to the persecuted Christian faith at the end of the third century. Even John Henry Newman had contributed to Wiseman's series, writing *Callista, A Tale of the Third Century*, which involved another beautiful convert renouncing love and enduring martyrdom for the sake of the faith.

None of these novels were very impressive as 'literature', Philip recognised. They were of interest primarily because of the way they manifested the ideology of their authors, both consciously and unconsciously. He became fascinated with Newman's other writing, especially his *University Sermons* and the book he published after finally converting to Roman Catholicism in 1845, *An Essay on the Development of Christian Doctrine*. Fourteen years before the publication of Darwin's *Origin of Species*, Newman argued that the Church, like any other human organisation, did not remain 'forever the same' but evolved over time. Also important to Philip's thesis were the books Newman wrote as a Catholic, such as the autobiographical *Apologia pro Vita Sua* and the *Grammar of Assent*, an attempt to describe in philosophical terms how it was that people came to faith. All these other writings helped to explain the underlying ideology of his novels. 'Ideology' was a word much in favour in the mid-1970s, especially in

Oxford, where one of the new appointments in the English faculty specialised in literary theory.

'Did you know he calls himself a Catholic Marxist?' one of Philip's friends whispered in the Bodleian Library when they observed him ordering some volumes there. The two of them looked on in awe as the bespectacled figure, wearing his trademark denims and beret, took his place in the Upper Reading Room. Philip, who was still grappling with Newman's understanding of what it meant to be a Catholic, was duly impressed. One of the issues addressed by Newman which resonated with Philip at this time was that of the authority of the Bible. Newman, like Philip himself, had experienced an evangelical conversion as a teenager but come to recognise that the Scriptures, to which evangelicals turned as the final arbiter of truth, were themselves in need of interpretation. A particular passage in the *Essay on Development* had seemed to leap out from the page when Philip first read it:

'We are told that God has spoken. Where? In a book? We have tried it, and it disappoints; it disappoints, that most holy and blessed gift, not from fault of its own, but because it is used for a purpose for which it was not given. The Ethiopian's reply, when St.Philip asked him if he understood what he was reading, is the voice of nature: "How can I, unless some man shall guide me?"'

Philip had quickly found the passage in the Acts of the Apostles which described St.Philip's encounter with an Ethiopian eunuch puzzling over the Book of Isaiah, unable to make sense of it. Only when St.Philip explained that it was Christ himself who had fulfilled the role of the suffering servant described by Isaiah could the eunuch comprehend its full meaning. For Newman this illustrated the point that the Bible was too complex to read without the services of an authoritative interpreter, in other words the Church.

Philip was pondering how to use this passage in his thesis while hurrying along the High Street one clear crisp autumn morning at the beginning of his second year as a postgraduate when he nearly bumped into a well-dressed clergyman in dog-collar and suit. Clerics were common enough in Oxford but Philip recoiled in surprise on seeing that the man to whom he had started apologising was none other than gorgeous George.

'What are you doing here?' Philip asked with his customary directness.

'I live here,' George replied, proceeding to explain that he had been appointed chaplain to one of the Oxford colleges and that Faith was training to become a teacher. 'We have a house in St.Aldate's which goes with the job. You must come round and visit, you and...'

'Rachel. We live in East Oxford.'

'Faith will be delighted to see you,' George insisted.

Philip was by no means sure that she would but he agreed all the same, partly out of curiosity. He wondered what Faith would make of Rachel, especially the fact that they were living together. The two men exchanged phone numbers and a fortnight later Philip and Rachel found themselves in St.Aldate's, just across from Tom Tower, ringing at their door.

'Should I talk posh?' Rachel asked as they waited for the door to open.

'No, just be yourself,' Philip had time to mutter before Faith was at the door, beaming at them both. She hugged Philip, which surprised him (maybe she had mellowed with marriage), before turning to Rachel.

'I've heard all about you from Philip,' Rachel began, somewhat inauspiciously.

'And what did he tell you?'

'Only the nicest things,' Philip assured her.

'And what are the nicest things about my wife?' came George's voice from within.

'Her smile?' suggested Philip.

'That will do,' Faith answered, ushering them into the living room, where they sat on a comfortable if somewhat battered sofa, opposite the fire. George brought them drinks while Rachel went through her usual routine on Verdi and Shakespeare. Philip too talked about his research.

'So you're succumbing to Newmania?' George prompted.

'I don't know about "succumbing",' countered Philip. 'I find him very interesting.'

'So we can expect you to follow him to Rome?'

'I'm not sure. I can see why he found the Anglican Church of his time unsatisfactory, too much part of the establishment, not so much a via media as a contradictory combination of Protestant theology and Catholic liturgy. He tried to make it more consistently catholic (with a small 'c') but after the rejection of Tract Ninety by the majority of his supposed co-religionists he was left with little choice but to leave.'

George explained for the benefit of the two girls, who were looking baffled, that Tract Ninety, one of a series of pamphlets produced by Newman and other members of the Oxford Movement in the 1830s and 40s was an ill-fated attempt to argue that the Thirty-Nine Articles, the litmus test of Anglican orthodoxy, were open to a catholic reading in spite of the Protestant intentions of their authors.

'Isn't that rather a difficult position to maintain?' Faith asked.

'Yes, it is,' Philip answered. 'It takes a fairly imaginative reading of the text to arrive there. Sometimes he sounds a bit like Stanley Fish, bamboozling his audience with a whole range of possible meanings to which the text is open.'

'Who on earth is Stanley Fish?' George asked, provoking a lengthy reply from Philip on Reader-Response Criticism, another product of contemporary literary theory now popular in his discipline.

'For Fish it's the reader in the end who decides on the meaning of any text. Transferred to the theological domain, it allows the "interpretive community" to decide how it wants to interpret a particular text. For Catholics that can mean the Church.'

'So Kingsley was right, then? Catholics don't really care for truth,' George argued.

'Well they do,' countered Philip. 'But they find it in and through the Church.'

'So you *are* going to convert?'

'As I said, I don't know. I go with Rachel to Blackfriars at the moment and find it frustrating not to be allowed to take communion. It would certainly help in that respect.'

'I didn't know you were a Catholic,' Faith said, turning to Rachel with her most charitable of looks, as if learning for the first time that she had inherited a fatal genetic disorder.

'Yes, from the cradle,' Rachel admitted. 'That means, of course, that I don't take it quite as seriously as Philip does.'

'Yes, he certainly does take things seriously,' Faith sighed, remembering some of their past arguments. But by this time the food was ready, so they all moved through to the dining room. Over the meal Faith talked about her experience of teaching and George talked about the undergraduates at his college, many of whom came from very privileged backgrounds.

'I've heard them called the cream of Oxford,' Philip laughed. 'Thick and rich.'

'Some of them are rich,' George agreed. 'And many

of them seem very thick-skinned. They don't seem to have any kind of social conscience. They splash money about as if it grew on trees.'

'For them it probably does,' Rachel interposed. 'Mind you, if you can't have a bit of fun when you're a student, I don't see when you ever will.'

'The problem with the Bullingdon Club,' Faith replied, 'is that their idea of fun is to throw other people's records into the pond.'

'Now that is a sin,' Rachel agreed. 'Unless they are poor recordings.'

Philip was enjoying the slight tension between the two women; it felt like the feminine equivalent of two men fighting over a woman. But when they got onto the subject of music, it transpired that they were both members of the Bach Choir and could swap stories about some of the recent concerts. They were soon, to Philip's surprise, treating each other as old friends and arranging to meet up for coffee during the week. This was something for which he hadn't bargained. He couldn't summon up the same enthusiasm for George, who was a little too clerical for his taste. The two couples, however, met at regular intervals to share meals.

The highlight of Philip's second year as a postgraduate was a conference he attended on Newman hosted by the International Centre of Newman Friends in Rome. He confessed to Rachel that he didn't feel quite ready to call himself a 'friend' of the deceased cardinal but was only too pleased to have an excuse to visit Rome. She was equally eager to return to Italy so the two of them spent the week before the conference touring the city together, combining his special interests (such as the catacombs) with hers (which included a visit to the Church of Sant'Andrea, the setting of the first act of Tosca). Philip humoured her by pretending to be the painter Cavaradossi comparing the diverse beauties of different women.

'You mean the austere beauty of Faith contrasting with my more sensual qualities,' Rachel laughed.

'You must admit that she is beautiful,' Philip replied.

'Oh yes, in that pure fashion that men like you and George seem to find irresistible.'

Philip let the comment go and they continued their tour of the city, ending with gelati in the Piazza Navona. On Easter Sunday they attended Mass in St.Peter's. Philip's initial reaction to its baroque splendours had been far from positive but now that it was packed with worshippers he found himself more impressed with its grandeur. They stayed in the square for the Pope's appearance on the balcony before heading off for more ice-cream.

'I can't say that I find the present Pope very exciting,' Philip confessed.

'That's all right, pet. He probably wouldn't care that much for you.'

That was about as far as their discussion of theological questions tended to go. Rachel had been brought up to take her faith for granted, not to interrogate it as Philip did. He could see that this gave her a sense of security which he lacked. At the same time, her lack of intellectual curiosity annoyed him.

Even Philip's taste for theological enquiry, however, was satisfied by the conference on Newman, which was attended by a wide range of the cardinal's 'friends', including Catholics and Anglicans, priests and lay people, academics and enthusiasts. The papers too varied from pious reflections on 'Newman and Providence' to impassioned pleas for academic freedom. There were keen reformers of the Catholic Church, fresh from the triumphs of the Second Vatican

Council, lining up against theological conservatives who insisted that the Council and Newman's supposed role in it had been much misinterpreted. Some of these seemed to regard Newman as a kind of Anglican Trojan horse, who had been wheeled within the gates of the eternal city only to disgorge radical ideas about the primacy of conscience and the role of the laity.

Many of the reforming theologians at the conference were German. Philip had some difficulty in following their papers, which were delivered in German, but in the bar afterwards, where they agreed to speak English, he heard much about the progressive views being propounded by Catholic theologians in both Holland and Germany. Among the latter was a man called Hans Küng, who had just published a controversial book, *On Being a* Christian, which proposed a rather different model of the faith from the neo-scholastic tradition still dominant in Rome. To follow Christ, according to Küng, was not to give assent to a series of propositions but to discover what it was to be fully human. This recognition of the limits of doctrinal formulae was something he shared with Newman.

Newman, Philip learnt from some of the theologians at the conference, had been one of the thinkers most frequently cited at the Second Vatican Council, particularly on the role of the laity and the development of doctrine. Philip had heard about the Council from Aidan but some of these theologians had actually been present as *periti* or experts. They were able to tell him about some of the events behind the scenes, the struggles between the 'progressive' theologians and the Curia, who tried unsuccessfully to limit the freedom the bishops had over the final form of the documents. He hadn't previously been aware of the role played by Pope Paul VI in the latter stages of the Council, when he had kept trying to smuggle additional phrases into documents already agreed. It gave him a new insight into the complex dynamics not only of the Council but of the Church as a whole, which was clearly not as monolithic as he had been led to believe.

Philip now became aware that his own contribution to the conference, a short paper on Newman's distinction between 'real' and 'notional' assent, on faith as an experience rather than a set of theological propositions, fitted rather well into this wider movement within the Church away from scholastic theology (with its belief in doctrines remaining forever the same) towards a more historical approach to the faith (as gradually evolving over time). Newman, for example, talked in the *Essay on Development* about Christianity as 'a fact in the world's history' rather than a 'dream of the study or cloister'. It had an 'objective existence' in the lives of individuals in history.

Philip argued that it was no accident that Newman turned to the novel as a form in which to represent the process of conversion both in the case of the third-century convert Callista and in Charles Reding, the hero of *Loss and Gain,* who had made the same difficult transition from Canterbury to Rome in the nineteenth century as Newman himself. A novel could describe what that felt like, giving imaginative substance to the whole process. Systematic theology, which dealt only with generalisations and abstractions, was less compelling in this respect, less 'real', more a matter of 'notions' (to use the cardinal's own terms). Not surprisingly, many of the theologians in his audience weren't altogether persuaded by this while the literary critics supported his argument enthusiastically.

There was a serious change taking place, Philip realised, in his own attitude towards Roman Catholicism as 'a fact in the world's history'. There might be aspects of the current teaching of the Catholic

Church that he found problematic, its attitude towards women and sexuality, for example. But these could change with time, as the recent Vatican Council had made clear. Doctrine, as Newman insisted, continued to develop as the believing community faced different challenges and acquired new insights. The Church of England meanwhile, seen from the vantage point of Rome, seemed a rather parochial off-shoot of history, an adaptation to particular historical contingencies (including the petulance of an over-lusty king) which seemed only temporary.

A not insignificant factor in his thinking, Philip realised, was that conversion to Rome would make marriage to Rachel that much more possible. Her parents were traditional Catholics who looked with disapproval on their current living arrangements. If they were to get married, however, they would certainly expect him to convert. This had previously been a cause of some anxiety on his part but he could now envisage a future for himself which would resolve both his religious and his personal difficulties. He could follow Newman into the Catholic Church.

Chapter 5

Rome

Rachel was delighted when Philip told her about his decision to convert, mainly because it would make relations with her family so much easier. He could now become 'one of them' rather than remaining aloof and critical. Her family already thought he was rather snobbish; at least wanting to become a Catholic showed he was trying to fit in. That Philip himself was serious about this (as about everything else) was apparent in the care he took over this process, receiving instruction from the Catholic Chaplain to the university throughout his third year as a postgraduate. Fortunately for him, Father Sean was an enthusiastic supporter of the reforms brought about by the Second Vatican Council, especially the ecumenism it recommended towards other denominations. He understood where Philip was coming from and the difficulties he would experience with some traditional Catholic practices and beliefs.

One of the ways in which Father Sean suggested that Philip might prepare for his reception into the Catholic Church was by reading some of the key documents of Vatican Two, which had recently been translated into English in a cheap paperback edition. They began with *Lumen Gentium,* whose Latin title, taken from its opening words (literally 'the Light of the World'), which Philip found considerably more attractive than to its stodgy English title, "Dogmatic Constitution of the Church". He liked its celebration of the 'charisms' of the laity, its description of all the baptised as 'the People of God', its recognition of the weaknesses as well as the strengths of the Church, which was 'at once holy and always in need of purification'. It was 'a Pilgrim Church', on a journey towards truth rather than claiming already to have found all the answers. The document acknowledged, for example, that it was not yet possible to give 'a complete doctrine of Mary', who remained part of the 'mystery of the Incarnate Word'. This appealed to Philip rather more than the certainty he had encountered in some old-school Catholics.

They went on to read *Gaudium et Spes* (literally 'Joy and Hope'), whose title was again rather more vivid in Latin than the English title "Pastoral Constitution on the Church in the Modern World". Father Sean explained that the word 'pastoral' was central to the whole document, focussing on the loving and healing relation between the Church and the world. The tone was set by its opening words, emphasising the solidarity of the Church with the whole human family: 'The joy and hope, the grief and anguish of the men of our time, especially of those who are afflicted in any way, are the joy and hope, the grief and anguish of the followers of Christ as well.' To become a member of the Catholic Church, as Father Sean explained, wasn't simply a matter of seeking salvation for oneself but of proclaiming the 'message of salvation intended for all men'. Philip couldn't help commenting on the absence of inclusive language here; 'women were human too,' he observed. He was impressed, however, by the way the document wrestled with what it called 'the crisis of growth', the rapid 'social and cultural transformation' taking place in the modern world. This had 'repercussions on the religious level' which the Church needed to address; it required a genuine dialogue with the modern world, 'listening to the many voices of our time', the 'ways of thinking and feeling as expressed in our culture'. That, Philip told Father Sean, was what his own discipline was about.

Father Sean himself was a keen student of Newman and was able therefore to take a genuine interest in Philip's research. For Philip in turn, having to explain Newman's fiction to someone well informed about his theology was a very useful exercise. He was now rewriting the introduction to his thesis, which entailed having to articulate the whole point of the enterprise. Father Sean was able to ask precisely the right question to force Philip to make this explicit. He could also point Philip in the direction of passages in some of Newman's more obscure sermons which helped to explain episodes in the novels. The two of them sometimes spent whole evenings together, surprised to find that several hours had passed without them noticing. Philip found these evenings rewarding both on a personal and a professional level.

Philip's formal reception into the Catholic Church took place in the summer of 1976 at the end of Philip's third year of research. It was a simple ceremony held, appropriately enough, in the recently completed Newman Building in St.Aldate's. A fairly small number of friends and family attended, including Aidan, who served as Philip's sponsor, and Rachel, of course, who came with her parents. Philip's parents were also present, although their bafflement by the whole process was obvious. The service was interrupted from time to time by the shouts and screams of some noisy Italian schoolchildren who were staying in the building on some kind of exchange. But since this brought back happy memories of Florence and Rome, even this had a certain appropriateness, reminding Philip that he was joining a living community, not just his (or Newman's) idea of a Church.

After the service they all repaired to an inn by the river, eating sandwiches in the garden among strutting peacocks and idling tourists. Rachel and Philip took the opportunity to explain their plans for the future to both sets of parents, who were meeting each other for the first time. Once he had submitted his thesis, he explained, he would be in a position to apply for academic jobs. Rachel was less far advanced with her thesis, which she hoped to complete wherever they eventually settled. She then planned to train as a teacher. All being well, they hoped to marry the following summer. If Philip failed to land a job in a university he too could train as a teacher. Meanwhile Rachel could always give flute lessons while he signed up as a tutor for one of the many cramming colleges in Oxford. They could survive, temporarily, on very little. Both sets of parents were reasonably happy with this, although they advised waiting until at least one of them had a 'proper job' before going ahead with the marriage.

Later that summer, after completing his thesis, Philip began the process of applying for posts. There was the inevitable delay before he heard anything in reply but at last he was summoned for interview for a lectureship in the Department of English Studies at Durham. He was extremely nervous about this but was helped by the fact that there was a theologian on the selection panel who asked the kind of questions about his research that Father Sean had already put to him. He was accordingly able to answer them with impressive fluency. He was offered the job that evening and had no hesitation in accepting. Rachel was delighted at returning to the North-east and together they set about looking for houses in Newcastle. What they could afford on Philip's starting salary was hardly grand but they eventually settled on a terrace house in the West

End of the city, not dissimilar to the one they had shared in Oxford.

The wedding took place in St.Mary's Cathedral in Newcastle, with its slender Gothic spire designed by Pugin. Rachel chose most of the music; she also insisted on reading Elizabeth Barrett Browning's sonnet, "How do I love thee? Let me count the ways!" Philip lectured her at length on the personal significance of the poem. When Barrett Browning swore, 'I love the with the passion put to use/In my old griefs,' he explained, she meant that she invested her love for her husband with the emotion expended on the death firstly of her mother and then of her favourite brother, for whose death she felt responsible. Did she really mean to use this rather sad metaphor of usury of their own love?

'Of course not, hun,' she replied. 'I just think it sounds nice.'

There was no arguing with this. Philip himself chose the more conventional passage on love from St.Paul's first letter to the Corinthians, drawing from Rachel the comment that she was glad he had recognised that love was greater than faith. Faith herself was there, of course, glowing with what appeared to be the first flush of pregnancy. The priest who celebrated the nuptial mass had accepted that Philip and Rachel did not themselves intend to have children straight away; so long as they intended eventually to have children, he insisted, it was all right. For a recent convert Philip realised he was being rather cavalier about the Vatican's teaching on birth control but he was quickly learning to draw the same distinction as cradle Catholics between the church's official line and what it tolerated pastorally. He told himself that it was only a matter of time, anyway, before the official teaching caught up with the actual practice of believers.

Philip learned quite a lot about the difference between theory and practice in his early years as a Catholic. 1978 was the year of the three Popes, Paul VI being succeeded first by John Paul I and then, some thirty days later, by John Paul II. Philip was pleasantly surprised to learn that the latter had written not only two doctorates but a number of plays and some verse. He struck a charismatic figure on the world stage, giving the Church a much more positive image. Even Philip's parents found his public persona engaging as he entered with gusto into a series of visits to all corners of the globe. It also helped, as far as Philip's father as concerned, that he had been a reasonably good goalkeeper.

The local parish church which Philip and Rachel attended, however, seemed to have changed little from the 1950s. Philip found that his role as a lay person was not, as Newman had suggested, to be consulted on matters of faith, but to think of as many ways as possible of making money. There seemed to be an endless round of fund-raising activities: bazaars, raffles, race-nights, music evenings, ceilidhs, plays and pantomimes, all of which called for talents he didn't possess. He did offer to read a few poems at a 'talent evening' but these were received with uncomprehending silence. He was recruited to play Santa Claus at the Christmas Bazaar, a role that he played with conscientious dedication, practising the exact tone of his chuckle before the mirror. But in trying to make the whole process educational, telling some of the older visitors to his grotto that the practice of exchanging gifts at Christmas originated in St.Nicholas's encouragement of donations to the poor, he once more miscalculated the effect on his audience. He was not invited to reprise the role the following year.

The preaching in the local parish church, too, was rather different from what he had encountered in Oxford. The priest, Father O'Connor, was a great believer in angels, who found their way into almost all of his sermons.

'Do you think he actually believes in all these angels?' Philip asked Rachel one Sunday.

'Well, he is Irish,' she replied.

'But what about the congregation. They didn't seem to bat an eyelid.'

'They probably weren't listening. And they're used to it. They would have heard even stranger things from the nuns at primary school.'

Philip could confess his reservations about angels to Rachel but decided that he had better keep his private thoughts from some of the others in the parish, including her family. This, however, left him feeling hypocritical and them thinking him reserved. Rachel's parents wondered why someone who talked for his living should be so silent with them. Her brothers too were offended by his persistent refusal to go drinking with them. He had told them that he needed a clear head for reading.

'Doesn't he do anything but work?' they asked Rachel.

'Not really,' she replied. 'We sometimes make love between books. It can be a bit uncomfortable, but we've got used to it.'

Rachel could joke about it but Philip's growing sense of isolation in the parish was becoming quite serious. There seemed to be no-one with whom he could discuss his difficulties with some traditional beliefs and practices. It came as a relief therefore to be invited by Faith and George to visit them at Cambridge for they, at least, would understand his difficulties. George, who had been appointed fellow-chaplain to one of the colleges, a post combining pastoral responsibilities with teaching and research, thought they might like to attend the inaugural lecture by the new Norris-Hulse Professor of Divinity, the first Catholic ever to be appointed to a chair in divinity at Cambridge. He too was a convert from Anglicanism, George told them. There wasn't room for them to stay in the small flat now dominated by their young children but there was a bed and breakfast just across the road where they would get a much better night's sleep.

Philip found the lecture itself both stimulating and reassuring, confirming that he wasn't alone in the kind of questions he asked. He was also pleased to hear references in it to some of the same critical theorists in which he was interested: Adorno, Horkheimer and Althusser. The lecture called for a 'critical theology' which would reflect, as in other disciplines, on the first-order language of the community of faith. This would lead to a less confidently systematic theology, less prone to absolute generalisations and more open to historical contingency, as befitted a religion which centred on incarnation. Such a theology, Philip was particularly pleased to hear, would be open to the writing of poets and novelists, whose work reflected such contingency.

'That was refreshing,' Philip commented as they made their way out of the auditorium.

'Most of it went over my head, I'm afraid,' Rachel admitted.

'As in everything else,' Philip explained, 'you have to be aware of the context. He's talking about a Church in which the dominant mode of doing theology is still neo-scholastic, producing huge systems of thought which are internally consistent but don't really engage with the world in which most people live. Even someone like Küng imagines himself to be producing a modern *Summa*, a modern version of Aquinas, that has answers to everything.'

'Isn't theology supposed to give answers?' Faith asked.

'Not all the time,' George replied. 'It should also ask questions, interrogating the language of faith, probing how it works.'

'That sounds painful,' Faith laughed. 'We have ways of making you talk more intelligently about God.'

'Well, that would be a good start,' Philip continued. 'You wouldn't believe the sort of language they use in our local church.'

'At least it's no longer Latin,' Rachel countered. 'Be thankful for small mercies.'

They had now reached George and Faith's flat, where the children quickly became the centre of attention. Thomas, who was just two, careered around the flat making engine noises, much to everyone's amusement, including his more sedate older sister Samantha, who was a year older.

'I'm Thomas the Tank Engine,' he explained.

'And do you want to have your language interrogated by theology?' Rachel asked. 'No, I didn't think so.'

'He does come out with some amazing words,' Faith told them. 'Sam too. They overhear their father and copy him, I suppose.'

George had managed by this time to catch Thomas and was trying to settle him down on the sofa. 'And what about you?' he asked. 'Any plans for children?'

'His children are his books,' Rachel moaned. 'He doesn't have the time for much else.'

'Or the energy,' Philip acknowledged.

'Well, don't leave it too late,' Faith warned. 'You'll have even less energy when you're older.'

The four adults then joined the children in a simple

supper before Faith and Rachel led them off to bed, leaving George and Philip in the living room, where their conversation, as usual, quickly turned to their research. George was working on a book on Augustine, which he explained at great length. Philip then outlined the plan of his current book, a study of George Eliot's fiction in the light of her translations of Spinoza, Feuerbach and Strauss. There had been some earlier critical work on the way Feuerbach's humanism filtered into her novels, he explained, but little on the other two.

'That's understandable,' George commented, puffing away at his newly-acquired pipe. 'Strauss is pretty hard going and probably doesn't seem that relevant to fiction.'

'But he is,' Philip exclaimed. 'That's the whole point. One of the criteria for detecting unhistorical elements in the gospels, according to Strauss, is the presence of "poetical" forms, which make them look too artful.'

'But you can write history "artfully",' George objected. 'Look at Gibbon or Carlyle.'

'I have,' moaned Philip. 'My supervisor suggested that I read *The French Revolution* to understand Victorian ideas of history.'

'And did it help?' George asked.

'Not much. It took me a fortnight to get through it and I was no wiser at the end.'

'And what about Strauss? Does he make you feel any wiser?'

'Not altogether. He's a thorough-going Hegelian, insisting that the supposed "facts" of the Christian faith are just symbols of a higher Idea, the spirit working itself out in history. "The Idea", he says, "is not wont to lavish all its fullness on one exemplar, and be niggardly towards others". It reveals the divine in the whole race of mankind rather than in one man. George Eliot liked that notion. Mind you, his relentless stripping away of all the poetic details of Christianity made even her "Strauss-sick". It took her two years to translate *The Life of Jesus*. You can't help admiring her persistence.'

'Also *his* courage and sincerity,' George added. '*The Life of Jesus* cost him his job.'

'He's very interesting on some things, for instance on myth, which he sees not as the opposite of historical truth but as a way of expressing deeper truths about history. In the case of the gospels he doesn't just dismiss the miracles out of hand or try to explain them "naturally". You know the sort of thing: Christ wasn't really walking on water but on a shelf of rocks just under the surface. The transfiguration was just a particularly bright ray of sunshine which happened to settle on Jesus. He rejects such earlier, supposedly scientific attempts to explain away the miracles, preferring to consider what the stories reveal about the beliefs of the earliest disciples. His account of the encounter on the Emmaus Road is especially convincing. He suggests that it dramatizes the way in which the disciples, devastated after the crucifixion by the destruction of all their hopes in a triumphant Messiah who would defeat the Romans, went back to the Hebrew Scriptures and discovered there the idea of a suffering Messiah. The whole story, he claims, dramatizes the psychological process of their reconciling themselves to his death.'

'I suppose so. The story doesn't make a lot of sense if you take it literally. I mean, why didn't the disciples recognise Jesus before he broke bread over the meal? What I find hard to take in Strauss is the relentless pursuit of supposed contradictions between the gospels. Who cares how many angels there were at the tomb? If you swallow one angel, you're not going to baulk at another account saying there were two.'

'Quite. I'm not too keen on any angels myself. But our priest is always going on about them.'

'Serves you right for becoming a Papist,' George laughed.

Philip too was able to laugh at this in spite of his very real difficulties. He was, like George Eliot herself, finding it hard to reconcile his intellectual agreement with Strauss's critical probing of the gospels with his own emotional attachment to them. What was actually left if you read all the miraculous elements within them as a 'mythological' expression of a poetic or philosophical truth? Wasn't it just a vague religious humanism of the kind George Eliot herself espoused? And what help was that in the face of all the suffering and injustice in the world? Eliot had talked of believing in the same Jesus, 'crucified and suffering rather than triumphant'. But that hadn't done much for her state of mind, leaving her lonely and depressed, unable to recapture the joy of her youthful faith. Philip was seriously worried that he might follow her in this respect. If it weren't for Rachel forever cajoling him out of introspection, he told George, the relentless dissection of the poetic details of the gospels would have made him Strauss-sick too.

Chapter 6

Durham

Back in the North-East Philip found himself living two
very different lives: that of academic routine, which
took over as soon as he reached the department in
Durham, and that of home, which centred mainly on
Rachel, her family and her friends. Some of her fellow-
musicians came round to practise and would stay for
drinks. Philip was always pleasant to them and did his
best to attend their concerts but they often clashed with
events linked to his academic life: lectures, discussion
groups, and social events at the university. Rachel
sometimes accompanied him to these but complained
when she did so that she hardly knew any of the people
there.

'If you came more often,' Philip objected, 'you
would get to know them better.'

'The same could be said of you and my friends,
hun.'

Even the term 'hun' had lost some of its attraction
for him, especially when it was used with a certain
element of irony, as on this occasion. Rachel was now
teaching music at a local comprehensive which made
increasing demands on her time. Philip would often
return from the university late at night, having left
home before she was awake. The fact that they did
fewer things together didn't escape the notice of her
family, her mother in particular.

'If you had children,' she told them, 'it would bring
you together more.'

'We have tried,' Rachel replied.

She had come off the pill a year or so after they first settled in Newcastle but now that she had a full-time post she wanted a few years' experience before taking time off. Philip, who had seen how happy George and Faith were with their children, would have preferred to start a family sooner rather than later. But he recognised Rachel's need to establish a career for herself, especially since his own was developing well. His book on George Eliot had been published by a major academic press and he had begun another on Newman. He enjoyed his teaching, which at Durham still involved one-to-one tutorials, a practice abandoned by many other English Departments. It demanded a great deal of time and effort (the constant re-reading of texts) but brought great satisfaction both to the student and to the teacher, who came to know each other extremely well. It helped Philip that most of his students were bright and attractive young women, whose admiration and respect boosted his fragile ego.

'I get older as the years go by,' one of his philandering colleagues had confided at a party, 'but the girls are always nineteen.'

Philip had been shocked at the time but had to acknowledge (to himself at least) that the company of intelligent young women was one of the perks of the job. He occasionally caught himself imagining afternoons with some of his favourite students similar to those he had enjoyed in Florence. But he made no attempts to put these dreams into practice and had secretly enjoyed the disgrace his lecherous colleague had suffered when one of the students with whom he had slept reported their encounter in gory detail in the student newspaper. This in turn had been picked up by *Spare Rib*, the feminist magazine, after which all lecturers in the department had been warned to behave in a more professional manner.

The fact that he saw so little of Rachel during the day helped for a time to keep the romance of their marriage alive. After spending their days apart, they returned to each other's arms at night with renewed enthusiasm. He told her about a student essay reported by a colleague in theology, in which Lot's wife had been called a pillar of cloud by day but a ball of fire at night.

'That's me, hun,' she laughed. 'But wasn't she turned into a pillar of salt?'

'Only for looking back,' he replied. 'Promise me that you will always look forward.'

'Yes, to our next holiday.'

The summer holidays they could now afford in Italy and Greece provided further opportunities to return to the idyllic conditions of their first summer together. But in Newcastle Rachel's family weren't alone in noticing the tensions between them. A woman from church recommended that they go on a marriage counselling weekend. These weekends, she explained, involved couples writing down what they had initially found attractive in their partners.

'I told her that if I wanted to write pornography,' Philip reported to Rachel that night as they lay in bed, 'I would do so in the comfort and privacy of my own home.'

'I don't think that's what she meant, pet. And besides, it's not just my body you should love me for.'

'Well, it's good place to start,' he replied, beginning to recite Swinburne:

'I have passed from the outermost portal
To the shrine where a sin is a prayer;
What care though the service be mortal?
O our Lady of Torture, what care?
All thine the last wine that I pour is,

The last in the chalice we drain,
O fierce and luxurious Dolores,
Our Lady of Pain.'

'So you'd like me a little fiercer, would you?'
Rachel laughed. 'I don't think Father O'Connor would
approve.'

Outside the bedroom, however, they didn't share
much. He had stopped discussing his work with her
since it became obvious that her interest in it was
minimal. He began one evening to tell her about some
useful contacts he had made in the theology department
at Durham.

'But aren't they all Anglicans?' she asked.

'Most of them, yes,' Philip had to admit. 'Does that
make a difference?'

'Of course it does, hun. Everyone knows that
Anglicans don't believe in anything.'

She wasn't totally serious about this, of course, but,
like most of the Catholics he had encountered, she took
no interest in recent theology. He worried about this,
anxious to bridge the gap between academic theology
and religious practice. He had tried to involve himself
more in the life of the local church, suggesting to the
priest that he might give a series of talks on the Bible as
literature, a subject on which there had been a number
of recent books.

Father O'Connor seemed puzzled, asking whether
calling the Bible literature meant that it wasn't true?

'Well, it comprises mainly of stories,' Philip pointed
out, 'much of whose meaning depends on the way they
are told, on their formal properties. And you can easily
miss those if you only read the short passages selected
for reading at Mass.'

'Give me an example.'

'Well, take the original ending of Mark's gospel at

chapter 16, verse 8, with the women who had seen the empty tomb saying nothing to anyone about it "for they were afraid". For one thing it's significant that the resurrection is first witnessed by women rather than men and for another, it begs the question how the rest of the disciples heard about the good news.'

'They must have heard about it somehow,' the priest insisted, 'or the Church wouldn't have got off the ground. Anyway, that's what the rest of the gospel recounts.'

'But that was probably added in the second century, to bring it in line with the other gospels.'

'How do you know that?'

'Some of the most ancient manuscripts end at 16:8,' Philip persisted. 'So unless you believe that Mark died after finishing verse eight, or the papyrus was cut off at that point, that is where he meant the story to end, forcing his readers to return from the world of the story to the actual world in which the good news about the resurrection had been passed on.'

'I could have told you that in the first place. You're just making it more complicated than it needs to be.'

Philip shrugged his shoulders and let it pass. Maybe this kind of literary analysis was just for academics. It was common in his rarefied circle to question the historicity of some of the 'events' recorded in the gospels. The quotation marks around the word 'event' signalled its problematic status, the impossibility of getting behind the beliefs of the early church to establish what had 'really happened', for instance at the resurrection. What was undeniable was that the disciples had been totally transformed by the experience. Philip himself worried that there was very little left of traditional Christian doctrine that the liberal wing of the Church of England didn't put in inverted commas. He hadn't yet become quite as postmodern as that himself.

What the official teaching of the Catholic Church was became a prominent issue in the summer of 1982 with the visit of Pope John Paul II to Britain. There was much speculation in the press about what he would say on the subject of birth control in particular. He was due to lead a large outdoor Service for the Family at Knavesmire race course near York on the Bank Holiday Monday at the end of May. Philip and Rachel, after much deliberation, decided to join the coach party from their own church that travelled there. The whole process of parking and making their way to their allotted positions in the racecourse took up an inordinate amount of time but eventually everyone was in place. The Pope himself arrived by helicopter from Manchester, where he had, among other things, met the Chief Rabbi, reaffirming the desire expressed at the Second Vatican Council for reconciliation between Christians and Jews. Philip was hoping that he might have something equally significant to say about the Church's teaching on sexuality.

The papal address began slowly with some references to 'the religious history of this part of England,' to St.Aidan and St.Cuthbert, the Venerable Bede and some of the martyrs of the Reformation. Pope John Paul then moved on to the subject of marriage, listing some of the positive elements in current attitudes to the subject: greater attention to 'the quality of interpersonal relationships' and to 'promoting the dignity of women'. Philip liked this and put his arm around Rachel's shoulder to signify his recognition of her dignity. He knew that there was going to be a negative side to the Pope's account of recent developments, however, and it came as no surprise that John Paul II should proceed to condemn both 'the scourge of abortion' and 'the spread of a contraceptive and anti-life mentality'. He went on to address married couples directly, citing St.Paul on the need to 'bear with one another...in kindness and humility, gentleness and patience'. Philip again glanced at Rachel, who returned his slightly questioning smile with a rather enigmatic one of her own. Some marriages, Pope John Paul accepted, were bound to fail, to break down irreparably, and those who suffered this should be treated with compassion and tolerance. But that shouldn't discourage the Church from continuing to uphold the ideal. This was reflected in the next part of the service, which involved a renewal of marriage vows in which both Rachel and Philip took part.

Afterwards, when they had returned to their coach, Philip couldn't help picking up on some of the phrases Pope John Paul had employed.

'You could argue that to dismiss a "contraceptive *mentality*" was actually a softening of Church teaching. You might, for example, decide to use contraception for a while but as long as you intended at some point to have children you could be said not to have a mentality opposed to life.'

'That's what we did, if you remember.'

'I've never really understood the distinction between "artificial" and "natural" when it comes to contraception,' he continued. 'After all, there's nothing very "natural" about the rhythm method, shoving thermometers up your arse and drawing charts. And you could argue that the scientific discoveries that have led to the development of the pill are based upon nature.'

'*You* could argue that, Philip, but I'm not sure anyone else would.'

Philip launched into an elaborate explanation of deconstruction, a reading strategy which involved the dismantling of such binary oppositions as nature versus culture. Western philosophy, according to the French philosopher Derrida, relied on such oppositions to fix meaning and make it stable. Literature, on the other hand, had always revelled in ambiguity, metaphor and other 'unstable' elements in language. That's why it had been literary critics who had been the first to join Derrida's deconstructive bandwagon.

'That's because you're all unstable, hun,' Rachel interrupted. 'Just a bunch of nutters.'

Philip reluctantly recognised her lack of interest in the subject and remained in silence for the rest of the return journey, limiting himself to occasional comments on the beauties of the North York Moors and of the sea glimpsed between cornfields and former pit villages.

'We should explore this coastline more,' Philip resumed. 'It looks interesting.'

Rachel yawned lukewarm agreement. That was another thing they didn't share, his enthusiasm for walking. He had wanted to buy a cottage in the Lake District, which was a fairly short drive away from them but she had thought the idea extravagant. They would never have time to visit it, she insisted, and were both hopeless with house maintenance. So they would have to spend a fortune on getting other people to look after it. Philip once more dropped the subject; there seemed little that he could talk about that she found of interest.

Philip realised that their marriage was hardly ideal but it came nevertheless as a severe shock when he returned from a conference in the States a few years after the papal visit to be told by Rachel that she had begun seeing someone else (another musician) and wanted to move in with him.

'But what about our recently renewed marriage vows?' he protested. 'You can't just leave me because you prefer someone else'

'Who says?'

'The Pope, for a start.'

'Since when did we pay any attention to him?'

'It's not just him, it's the whole Church. And anyway, I thought you loved me.'

'I did,' she replied. 'But I don't any longer. And you don't really care about me, not about any of the things that matter to me, my music, for example.'

'You don't exactly take much interest in my work,' he countered.

'Precisely. We've grown apart. And we never really shared anything anyway apart from our bed. With Tony it's different.'

'And who's Tony when he's around?'

Rachel explained that he was another flautist who played in the same orchestra as her. He was the director of a local company with a large house on the outskirts of the city into which she intended to move as soon as possible. Philip could keep their house and, since there were no children involved, the whole thing would be relatively painless.

'What about my pain?' he asked, realising that he sounded ridiculous.

'You can pray to Our Lady of Pain,' she mocked. 'Let's see if she comes to your aid.'

Rachel hadn't expected Philip to react quite so strongly. But for him it was as if lightning had struck twice, first with Faith and now with Rachel. He had been confident in both cases that they loved him, only to find that they had turned to someone else. Was he so unlovable? The question, or rather the implied answer, sent him spiralling into depression. He found himself unable to get up in the mornings, lying in bed unable to muster sufficient energy to perform the simplest of tasks. Rachel became seriously worried about him, coming round daily to make sure that he was all right and that he had something to eat. Fortunately, he had been allotted a sabbatical term for research, so his absence from the department wasn't noticed. But it was clear that he needed help.

Rachel contacted Faith to let her know how poorly Philip was, wondering whether he could stay with them in Cambridge for a while. The change of scene would do him good and he could pursue his research in the library there, giving him something to do. The children too might take him out of himself. Faith, as ever, was sympathetic, though George needed some persuading. A fortnight later, however, Philip found himself installed in the spare bedroom of their new house, the subject of some puzzlement on the part of the children.

'Why is Uncle Philip so sad?' Thomas asked his mother one morning after breakfast. He was now a precocious eight-year-old.

'Because he's had a nasty shock,' Faith explained.

'What kind of a shock? An electric shock?'

'No, an emotional one.'

'How can you have an emotional shock?' Tom persisted.

'When someone you love betrays you,' Philip answered, having heard the last part of the conversation as he came downstairs.

'What do you mean by betray?'

'When she fucks off with someone else,' Philip answered. There was a shocked silence as both Faith and the children took this in.

'He said the F word,' Thomas chortled, while Samantha, who was now nine, went bright red. Philip apologised and breakfast continued as if nothing had happened. Faith, however, returned to the subject after taking the children to school.

'You should be more careful about what you say to the children,' she began.

'Yes, I'm sorry. It's not really me.'

'Or maybe it *is* you but not a part of yourself that you like.'

'Spare me your amateur psychology,' he snapped.

'Well, if you don't want my "amateur" help, perhaps you should try a professional.'

'To be honest, I'll consider anything.'

'George could put you in touch with someone here. He often refers students to counsellors.'

'I'd rather go through my G.P., if you don't mind.' Philip didn't want to be indebted to George for anything.

'Suit yourself. You normally do.'

When he returned to Newcastle later that summer Philip forced himself to see his G.P., who referred him to a consultant psychiatrist. She assured him there was very little likelihood of one-to-one sessions on the N.H.S. but recommended a friend of hers, who would probably be able to take him on immediately as a private patient. Philip couldn't avoid chuckling when he was given her name.

'Amanda. She who has to be loved. It gets better and better.'

'Well, if *you* are to get better,' came the reply, 'you could use her help.'

Philip accordingly rang the number he was given and arranged for a preliminary meeting with Amanda, who styled herself a psychiatric psychotherapist. After explaining what this actually meant, she offered Philip weekly sessions with her. He wasn't at all sure what he had let himself in for but was prepared at this stage to try anything that might help him feel less miserable.

Chapter 7

Confession

Driving to see Amanda once a week at her house on the outskirts of Morpeth became part of Philip's routine for the next few years, the half-hour journey there and back being part of the process, helping him to prepare for and reflect on the hour's session itself. Not that Amanda would let him begin where he wanted or speak to some pre-ordained script. One of his problems, she told him, with the emphasis on *one,* was a desire to control everything, especially his feelings, to avoid being caught by surprise.

'You have to let go more,' she told him at one of their early meetings, 'to let things happen.'

'But it's what happened that got me here,' he complained.

'I don't think it just happened, Philip. It was coming for quite a long time.'

They began with his present predicament, the fact that Rachel had left him. Amanda asked why he thought she had done that.

'I don't know. She just fell for someone else.'

'But why was she open to another relationship?'

'Well, I suppose she wasn't satisfied with ours.'

'And why do you "suppose" that was?' Amanda asked, a hint of exasperation in her voice. Some mornings he was hard going, answering in short sentences or even monosyllables. He knew what she wanted him to say, or thought he did, and refused to go along with it. His resistance was palpable in the way he had to force the words out of his mouth.

'Well, I *suppose* we didn't share enough, didn't talk enough, didn't do enough together. But that didn't seem to matter before.'

'Before what?'

'Before she left me.' This time it was Philip's voice which betrayed his irritation.

'But we need to go further back than that, to try to establish *why* she left you. Or perhaps further back still, to the time when you first fell in love with her. Why *did* you love her, do you think?'

'She was gorgeous!' Philip exclaimed, recalling their first encounter in Florence. 'She had freckles, short black hair, a lovely tan, a great figure...'

'Okay, I don't need a complete inventory. You're saying that it was her looks that first drew you to her?'

'I suppose so. But she also had an infectious laugh. She was fun to be with.'

'Fun?'

'Yes, in those days I was capable of fun, or at least of liking it in others.' There was a slight pause as they both reflected on the way this had come out.

'So you don't have fun on your own?'

'Not since I married,' Philip laughed, his dirty laugh, loud and over-confident. Amanda was not amused.

'Why is it that you always associate Rachel with sex?' she asked.

'Well, she was the first woman I ever slept with,' came the reply.

'How old were you?'

'Twenty, or twenty-one. I was pretty desperate, I can tell you.' Philip went on to explain the difficulties he had encountered in his relationship with Faith.

'So you think that she was frigid?'

'Perhaps not frigid, but she was very strict in terms of what she would let me do.' There was another pause as they both pondered this.

'Why do you think that was?' Amanda asked. 'Might she have thought you wanted "it" (sex) rather than her?'

'Possibly,' Philip admitted. 'Don't forget I was at an all-boys boarding school. I didn't know what a girl was.'

They talked for some time about his experiences at school, in particular his attraction to some of the other boys. Philip insisted that they were 'substitute girls', the nearest he was allowed to the real thing. But he had to admit that his feelings about them had been fierce and that they had often dominated his thoughts. A fleeting smile from one of the boys on which he had been temporarily fixated would light up his whole day.

'You say "boys". Were there lots of them?'

'Not that many,' Philip answered. 'And not more than one at a time. And there was the occasional girl, especially in primary school and later on in the holidays. Often I wouldn't even know who they were but just saw them, for instance in the street when I was staying with my grandparents.'

'Didn't you ever tell anyone about your feelings?' asked Amanda.

'No, I was ashamed of them. I thought they weren't "normal".'

'Even your feelings for some of the girls?'

Philip thought about it. He recalled one particular time when a girl at his primary school to whom he had been attracted had been found 'trespassing' in the gardens behind the row of army houses where they lived. She had claimed that Philip had invited her so she had been brought to their front door to confirm if this were true. Confronted by his father, Philip had denied knowing her altogether. Even retelling the episode after a gap of twenty years made him blush with shame.

'Why do you think you did that?' Amanda asked.

'I really don't know, even now. I seem to have been ashamed of my feelings for her. She was pretty, with blonde curly hair. Everyone at school knew that I had a crush on her but I never told my parents about her.'

'Why not?'

'Well, we weren't exactly encouraged to talk about our feelings. There were a lot of things I felt I couldn't tell my parents, for instance the fact that the headmaster of the school had made a pet of me. He would call me out of class to help in his office and when I was there would hug and kiss me.'

'You mean that he abused you?'

'If that's what you want to call it. He didn't do anything grossly sexual but I can see now that what he did was inappropriate.'

'What about then? What did you think of it at the time?'

'I don't know.' Philip tried to get back into the thoughts and feelings of his nine-year-old self. 'I remember that I didn't like it, feeling the bristles of his chin on my cheek. And I must have realised that this was unusual; he didn't behave like this with other children. The other teachers must have suspected that something was going on but they just let it go, as I did, not wanting to make a fuss.'

'Make a fuss!' Amanda exploded. 'This man was abusing you and you didn't want to make a fuss?'

'Well, I didn't know it was called abuse. No-one talked about things like that in those days.'

'So you said nothing to anyone?'

'No, not until today. There was no-one I felt I could talk to.'

'Not even your mother?'

Philip thought about this. He had been close to his

100

mother in those early years at primary school. He remembered how he used to rush back home at midday, gulp down the food she had prepared and then run straight back to school so he wouldn't miss out on the football game in the yard. At the end of the day, when he had his bath, he used to tell her about some of the things that had happened at school. But it was always an edited version of the day's events, omitting anything she wouldn't have wanted to hear. Similarly, when he went to football matches with his father, anything he told him always had to be positive. He had understood from an early age that he was supposed to be successful.

This tendency to suppress anything smacking of weakness or failure, he now saw, had become even more exaggerated at boarding school. He remembered vividly how his mother had flown back with him from Singapore to see him 'settled' at the new school. They had bought his uniform, stiff shirts with uncomfortable detachable collars, long grey flannel trousers and jacket. He hardly recognised himself in the mirror of the school shop. Then suddenly she was gone. He had known for some time that this was going to happen, that he was going to be left to fend for himself, but it only became real to him on the day she flew back to Singapore. It was the sheer distance, the impossibility of seeing her again until the following summer, that had got to him. He told Amanda how he had suddenly been overcome by feelings of loss; desperate not to be seen in this state, he had taken refuge in the laundry room.

'So you quite literally hid your feelings.'

'Yes. I knew that I didn't want to see anyone; I didn't want any of the other boys to know how I felt. Then one of the teachers found me.'

'What did he do?'

'He was quite nice to begin with, asking me questions about my parents, what it was like in Singapore and so on. But the only piece of advice he gave me was to keep a stiff upper lip.'

'Very public school!' Amanda snorted. 'And I suppose you did.'

'Yes. I remember writing home about all the good things at school, how I was taking to rugby like a true hero although I didn't actually enjoy it very much. I drew diagrams of the tries I scored, indicating the exact spot on the pitch from which I had received the ball and where I touched it down. I didn't tell them that I had broken down in tears during a history lesson when some ink spilt onto my exercise book.'

'What happened then, when you cried in class?'

'The teacher was quite sympathetic, which surprised me, since I was scared stiff of him. He had steel tips on his shoes which made a huge noise when he strode along the corridors. We would all go silent when he approached. On that occasion, though, he was all right.'

'But did anything change as a result?'

'Not that I noticed. He might have said something to my housemaster. But if he did, nothing was ever said to me or, as far as I know, to my parents. They were several thousand miles away.'

'And you didn't say anything at all to them, even when you saw them?'

'No. I didn't see them until the following summer anyway. In those days the army only paid for one return flight a year for children to rejoin their parents. Some parents, I would later discover, paid out of their own pockets for their children to see them more often. Now, of course, I wonder why my parents didn't make that effort, expensive though it would have been. But in those days I didn't question their decisions; I just accepted them. By the time I did eventually see them the following summer I had toughened up considerably, at least on the outside. I remember my mother wanting to help with something – I'm not sure what - and me saying that I could do it myself. She was quite upset, I recall: "Aren't we independent?" she mocked.'

Philip stopped at this point, surprised by the strength of his feeling about this, so long after the event. Amanda let him dwell on it for a while before resuming.

'Weren't you ever angry with your parents for sending you away?'

'Not at the time. I knew they wanted the best education for me and I was at a school widely regarded as one of the best in London. Academically, at least. Mind you, I remember them arguing about whether I should go there. My mother wasn't at all keen on the idea but let herself be persuaded by my father. To be fair, the alternative wasn't that attractive. If I hadn't gone there, I would have trailed around the world after my father, going to a whole range of different schools, as my sisters did.'

'But you would have been with your family.'

'That hadn't done me much good up to then. But I suppose I bottled things up even more at boarding school. My friends complained I went around looking worried most of the time. And I did worry about the smallest things. I remember getting into a state of anxiety over the damage I had done to my copy of Verdi's Requiem, which we were singing in choir. The director of the choir had impressed upon us the importance of looking after them properly. Somehow I had managed to tear one of the pages. It was weeks before I plucked up the courage to tell anyone.'

'And who did you tell?'

'Another music teacher, who also taught me Greek. We all thought him a bit "soft", which is presumably why I felt I could turn to him. He helped me to patch the page up with sellotape.'

'Well, that fixed the tear on your page. Do you think he saw the one in your heart?'

'Probably not. That wasn't in his job description.'

'I don't know how you survived.'

'I'm not sure that I did. Part of me didn't, anyway, the part that's supposed to feel emotions, share them with others, trust people and so on. Is it too late to learn this now?' Philip put on his 'silly' voice: 'Can you cure me, doctor?'

Amanda laughed. 'You have to cure yourself. But I can help.'

So the sessions continued, taking Philip back to his earliest memories, when they had lived in a remote house in the countryside. He recalled making mud pies for the cows while his mother did the domestic chores. He had been left very much to himself in those early days, long before nurseries had been invented. He hadn't really learnt to 'socialise' with other children until infant school. Then, just when he felt settled there, his father had been moved to London and so he had to start all over again at a new school. He remembered the sheer panic that had overcome him on being confronted with a sea of strange faces. He hadn't been able to breathe properly. The teacher thought he might suffer from asthma and had called his parents. They insisted there was nothing wrong and later, when they returned home, told him off for making such a fuss.

'Are you sure about that?' Amanda asked. 'Didn't they show any concern for you?'

'To be honest, I can't remember exactly what they said. All I know is that it felt as if it were my fault for making such a song and dance about changing schools.'

A number of such memories came back to Philip as he talked to Amanda, enabling him to construct an alternative narrative of his schooldays to the earlier chronicle of sporting and academic achievements. He wasn't sure, however, that he liked this alternative narrative any better, this sad series of painful episodes recovered from the recesses of his memory. After one particularly harrowing session, he came to the conclusion that he was so repressed and incapable of feeling that he was almost autistic. Perhaps that was why he made such a successful academic, living in his own little world, making the publishing equivalent of mud pies. His self-esteem reached an all-time low. He knew that Freud had famously said that he didn't promise to make people happy, only to help them discover why they weren't. But that wasn't of much comfort to him now.

Another aspect of Freud's thinking of which he was aware was the process of transference, the patient's projection of feelings for other people onto the analyst. He hadn't initially found Amanda that attractive, in spite of his joke about her name. She was an extremely serious woman, rarely smiling or showing much in the way of emotion. But she had a keen intelligence, remembering absolutely everything that he told her. She had a good figure too, he noticed. In the winter, she would light a coal fire in the room where they held their sessions and Philip started to fantasise about their making love on the rug in front of the fire. He wondered if he should tell her but kept on putting it off until one day an opportunity to do so arose.

They had been discussing his feelings for one of his female colleagues, a spectacularly intelligent young woman with boyish short hair and a clear complexion; just his type. Amanda had asked him what he imagined himself doing with her. Philip at first made a joke about cunnilingus, that he had always thought it was an Irish ferry service until he had read Swinburne. Since

Amanda seemed to have found this genuinely amusing, he decided to take the plunge and ask what the limits of their own relationship were.

'What do you mean?' she asked.

'Well, are we allowed to do anything physically?'

'You mean sexually?' Amanda asked. 'No, we aren't. That would be unprofessional.'

'Because you would be taking advantage of a vulnerable person, a patient?'

'Yes, it would be like you sleeping with one of your students.'

Philip said that some of his colleagues hadn't found this a barrier. It was clear, however, that Amanda would not consider any kind of physical relationship between them and so the sessions continued with Philip gradually abandoning his fantasies about her. But he looked forward every week to his session with her and began slowly to improve. Now that his sabbatical was over, the regular contact with students also helped his recovery. Few people, in fact, realised how ill he had been. His increased understanding of his own feelings in fact seemed to help with his teaching. He became more sensitive to the feelings of his students, more aware too of the psychological dimension of some of the texts he studied.

Philip's increased attention to the emotional level of reading also affected his research. He began looking at some of his favourite writers differently. He gave a paper to a conference on Newman in which he noted the tensions within the cardinal's attitude to language. On the one hand he had a very Romantic view of literature, the subjective or personal use of language to express feelings. Poetry, for example, he described in an early essay as 'the free and unfettered effusions of genius'. But the fact that it was 'unfettered' left it open to the waywardness of man's sinful nature. Literature, he later wrote became a place for 'the plungings and the snorting, the sporting and the buffooning, the clumsy play and the aimless toil of the noble, lawless savage'. It expressed 'not objective truth...but subjective', lacking the discipline of grace.

Philip proceeded to relate this to the tensions within Newman himself between his powerful personal feelings and the discipline he tried to impose upon them. Philip questioned whether it was possible ever to subject language to complete control. He related Newman's binary opposition between 'objective' theology and 'subjective' literature to that more widespread cultural opposition between 'masculine' reason and 'feminine' emotion. It was men, after all, who attempted to impose control over the thinking of the Church, excluding 'female' tendencies towards the supposedly irrational and subjective. It was men too who regarded women as unclean, associated with the flesh.

Philip hadn't initially intended the discussion to go in this direction. But he had begun to see that questions of gender had a tendency to encroach on any topic. The attempt to 'keep them out' (both feelings and women) was symptomatic of the problem that plagued institutions as well as many individuals. It was also, Philip recognised, what he had tried to do with his own feelings back in school. Feelings were messy; they disturbed you and prevented you from working properly. Best therefore to keep them at bay. Only it hadn't worked, this strategy, either on a personal or an institutional level.

Things were beginning to change, however. In universities, for example, women had already succeeded in breaking down some of the barriers that men had tried to keep in place. Many departments, including his own, were now being run by women, much to the discomfort of some of his older male colleagues. A majority of the students, as ever, were female but it had begun to look increasingly absurd that most of the staff were male. Conventional value judgments about literature which had produced a largely male canon of poetry had also begun to appear rather ridiculous, a product not of 'objective' values but 'subjective' prejudices. The syllabus therefore had begun to change. Students were demanding to read more women writers while publishers were wanting editions of previously neglected work by women. It was becoming a very different world from the one in which he had grown up.

Chapter 8

Fall

One of the people who helped Philip adjust to this new world was Faith, who had herself discovered feminism in the 1970s when it began to impinge on theology. She was now teaching Religious Studies in a sixth-form college in Cambridge, a place with a strong academic reputation sometimes attributed to the number of dons' children who attended. Philip continued to visit them as often as he felt possible without imposing too much on George's good nature. Faith's support, of course, he took for granted. He particularly liked visiting Cambridge in the spring or early summer, when the Backs were at their best. There were always some rare books or manuscripts in the University Library which he could claim it was essential for him to consult.

Philip recalled one particular evening in the late 1980s when he had finished reading the Acton papers (which contained some interesting comments on Newman) and returned from the library slightly earlier than normal to find Faith working in her study typing away furiously. He waited for her to finish, taking the opportunity to browse through some of the books on her shelves. He could remember even at a distance of over twenty years how taken aback he had been at some of the titles: one volume claimed to go *Beyond God the Father*, another celebrated *The Motherhood of God*, while a third deplored *Sexism and God-Talk*. Several shelves seemed to be given up to books of this kind, offering a radical challenge to patriarchy. Most, he noticed, were the products of the last decade. He couldn't resist making some reference to their contents.

'That's a frightening array of books you've got there. You'd have thought God the Father might have called it a day.'

'Or at least changed His name,' Faith laughed. 'Not all of these writers actually call for His resignation. They merely want us to recognise that His gender is only a metaphor. Many of them remain within the Christian tradition. Rosemary Radford Ruether, for example, sees herself as revising rather than rejecting Christianity.'

Philip had picked up a volume entitled *Womanspirit Rising* and was flicking through its pages with a look of distaste. He read aloud one of its chapter titles, 'Why Women Need the Goddess.'

'That's by Carol Christ,' Faith explained. 'And yes, that *is* her name. She's definitely one of the post-Christians.'

'I suppose we're all post-something these days. And who is the Goddess?'

'It's not any particular Goddess. It's more of a generic term signalling the need for us to learn from other cultures which had goddesses. The problem with traditional Christianity is that it doesn't make much allowance for the feminine. You have a male Father, a male Son and a Spirit who is at best gender-neutral. There's Mary, of course, but she's traditionally seen as a model of feminine passivity and obedience, which is hardly what we want.'

'Isn't that just a product of the historical character of Christianity? Everything was male-dominated in the period during which it arose.'

'Not just then,' Faith retorted. 'The question now is whether we abandon the whole of Christianity as irredeemably flawed or "correct" it. We can't just accept the tradition as it stands.'

'But how far does this "correction" go?'

'Well, opinion on that varies. Someone like Elizabeth Schüssler Fiorenza remains a Catholic, you'll be pleased to hear. Her book *In Memory of Her* sees her task as a matter of recognising the message of liberation that Christianity originally brought – for women as well as men. Hence her subtitle, *A Feminist Theological Reconstruction of Christian Origins*. The feminism is there in the founding texts, she claims, especially in the gospels, but has been obscured by centuries of patriarchal interpretation. It's time for women to rediscover the original message.'

'People are always talking of getting back to the original message, before it was corrupted.'

'That's not what Rosemary Radford Ruether does – she was also brought up a Catholic by the way. She says that all religions need constant revising in the light of current experience. That's what the Reformation was about: an ironing out of some of the corruptions of the Church.'

'That's a nice feminine metaphor,' Philip interrupted.

'Only because most men can't be bothered to do their ironing. Anyway, it's not just a negative thing. Ruether suggests we should also add to the tradition, incorporating material from whatever seems of value in contemporary culture. Classical theology did so in the past, Aquinas incorporating elements of Aristotle, for example, so there's no reason why we shouldn't continue to do so.'

'But on what grounds?' Philip asked. 'Who is to say what's worthy of inclusion and what isn't?'

'That's a good question. Ruether's basic principle, her "golden thread", by which all elements of the tradition should be judged, is whatever allows rather than denies the full equality of women.'

'Then there must be a large part of the tradition that she wants to change.'

'Yes there is,' Faith laughed. 'You sometimes wonder what will be left. The demonization of Eve and the whole doctrine of the Fall get an absolute hammering, as you might expect.'

'Did someone mention the Fall?' came a voice from the stairs. It was George, returning from a particularly boring faculty meeting. He treated them to a quick summary of its more absurd moments before Faith explained that she had been giving Philip a quick seminar on contemporary feminist theology.

'Then he'll need a stiff drink!'

George opened a bottle of wine in the kitchen and began preparing some pasta. He also reminded them that they had promised to attend a seminar of the Patristics Group that evening on the subject of the Fall. One of his postgraduates was presenting a paper on why Augustine succeeded in carrying the day against the British theologian Pelagius and other opponents of the new doctrine. George, who was a regular at this particular group, could hardly miss a paper by one of his own students. Faith too was keen to attend so Philip had little option but to accompany them.

'Edward's only in the first year of his Ph.D.,' George explained. 'His paper addresses some of the arguments in a new book by Elaine Pagels.'

'Isn't that the woman who wrote the book on *The Gnostic Gospels*?' Philip asked, reminding Faith of that holiday in the Lake District when Aidan had talked of little else.

'She also discusses them in her new book,' George continued. 'Mainly in terms of their readings of Genesis. She goes on to argue that Augustine's doctrine of original sin was quick to gain acceptance because it met the needs of contemporary ecclesiastical politics. It appealed to the newly established imperial Church of the fourth century because a fallen humanity could be seen to need the discipline and control that the Church wanted to wield. That's a bit an oversimplification, of course, but you'll hear more tonight. There's also quite a lot about sex, you'll be pleased to hear.'

'Is it true,' Philip asked, 'that Augustine regarded erections as a proof of original sin?'

'Yes, especially the fact that you can't control when you have them; they come when you don't want them and don't come when you do.'

'Ah yes, we all know that problem,' Philip laughed.

Philip was surprised to find that Faith laughed too. She had clearly moved on from the puritanical young girl who had rejected his clumsy advances. She was also more confident in other respects, for instance in the way she dealt with Tom and Samantha, who were now mature enough to be left alone for the evening when the three adults made their way to the Divinity Faculty for the seminar.

Edward, whom they met briefly before the seminar began, proved to be a rather shy young man with unkempt hair and spectacles. He began his paper by summarising Augustine's discussion of the Fall in the *City of God*, where the loss of control over the body (including its erections) and general shame about sex was identified as part of the punishment meted out to Adam and Eve as a result of their 'disobedience'. In Genesis 3:16, Augustine noted, Eve had been cursed not only with the pains of childbirth but with 'desire' for her husband. This notion of sexual desire as a punishment was central to Augustine's reading of Genesis. Sex, in his view, became the very vehicle through which original sin was passed down (through the semen).

The British monk Pelagius, Edward continued, had

been somewhat dismayed by this dark new direction in which Augustine was trying to take Christianity. For Pelagius nature remained good, the gift of a generous God, and human beings were free to choose good rather than evil. His cause was taken up by an Italian bishop, Julian of Eclanum, who also insisted that everything created was good, including the body (and therefore sex). Julian rejected the idea that the structure of the universe had changed as the result of one man's transgression. Although his arguments only survived as cited by Augustine, the quotations were substantial enough to give a good indication of his argument. While Julian saw the world in a positive light, Augustine portrayed men and women everywhere (here Edward waggled his fingers to indicate an extended quotation which he read with growing relish) as 'struggling against human desire; pregnant women, nauseated, pale, unable to tolerate nourishment; others in labour, pouring forth immature foetuses in miscarriage; others, groaning and screaming in labour'. So much for the supposedly paradisal world celebrated by the Pelagians.

The audience, which had begun to titter at the description of the horrors of labour, was stunned into silence by Augustine's list of the other evils in the world: disease and death, 'bereavements and mournings everywhere'. The question, Edward concluded, was whether Pagels was right to see this as politically motivated, a depraved human nature requiring the control and discipline of the Church, or whether Augustine's was a more accurate reading both of scripture and of the world. He personally had some sympathy with Augustine's position, for which recent history provided ample evidence. And while Augustine's horror at sexuality might appear extreme, it was hard to deny that desire could take evil forms.

Edward finished the paper a little sheepishly, aware that he was challenging the politically correct tendency to denounce Augustine as irredeemably misogynist. Among the questions addressed to him, as George had warned him to expect, were a number citing some of Augustine's less sympathetic comments on women. Faith herself quoted his denial that women on their own bore the image of God, his insistence that it was only by grace, by overcoming the flesh and living in the spirit that they could attain salvation. In this, Edward replied, Augustine was clearly following St.Paul, who was equally suspicious of the flesh. A similarly ascetic strain ran through the teaching of Christ himself so Augustine could hardly be accused of novelty in this respect. The discussion remained amicable, however, not only in the seminar itself but afterwards, when George invited Edward home for drinks. While George was pouring these, Philip told Edward that the passage from Augustine on the prevalence of sin and suffering in the world reminded him of a similar passage in Newman's *Apologia*.

'I've got a copy of that on my desk,' George shouted from the kitchen. 'Why don't you fetch it and read us the passage?'

Philip, who needed no second invitation, quickly found the quotation, which he proceeded to declaim to the company at large in as grandiloquent a tone as he could muster:

'To consider the world in its length and breadth, its various history, the many races of man, their starts, their fortunes, their mutual alienation, their conflicts... , the blind evolution of what turn out to be great powers or truth...the greatness and littleness of man, his far-reaching aims, his short duration, the curtain hung over his futurity, the disappointments of life, the defeat of good, the success of evil, physical pain, mental anguish, the prevalence and intensity of sin, the pervading idolatries, the corruptions, the dreary hopeless irreligion, that condition of the whole race, so fearfully yet exactly described in the Apostle's words, "having no hope and without God in the world" – all this is a vision to dizzy and appal; and inflicts upon the mind the sense of a profound mystery, which is absolutely beyond human solution.'

'They don't write sentences like that any more,' Edward commented.

'Thank God,' said Faith.

'Anyway,' Philip resumed, returning to his normal voice, 'as a result of this painful condition, Newman goes on to argue that the human race must be involved in "some terrible aboriginal calamity" which theologians call "original sin".'

'So you have to be a pessimist to be a Christian?' Faith asked.

'Just a realist,' Philip answered, 'at least about human nature.'

'Actually,' Faith continued, 'it's not the grim view of life offered by these grumpy old men that I object to so much as the misogyny, the blaming of women for the miseries of life.'

'But that was a commonplace of the time,' George objected. 'Epiphanes called women "a feeble race". Tertullian, a century earlier, suggested they were "the devil's gateway". Even those Fathers who appeared to like women, such as Jerome, insisted that they abstain from sex.'

'All the more reason for us to be critical of the tradition,' Faith insisted.

'Like your feminist theologians of yours are doing?' Philip asked.

'Only they're not simply negative. You should read Schüssler Fiorenza on the gospels, which are actually very positive about women.'

Philip remained unconvinced, provoking a brief summary from Faith of the way both Mark and John portrayed the women disciples in a much more positive light than the men. In Mark, for example, the male disciples were forever failing to understand Jesus. They bickered about who was going to take precedence in the kingdom. They betrayed him (in the case of Judas), denied him (in the case of Peter) and abandoned him altogether at the crucifixion. Only the women remained loyal, anointing him for burial and watching where he was laid. They were then, of course, the first to be told of the resurrection. It was a similar story in John's Gospel, which began (after its meditative prologue) with Mary telling people to do what her son says at the wedding in Cana and continued with Jesus paying what the male disciples clearly thought was unwarranted attention to the Samaritan woman at the well. Mary of Bethany and her sister Martha occupied key roles in the developing story while Mary of Magdala was the first actually to meet the risen Lord.

'It's astonishing how much prominence women are given in the narrative,' Faith concluded, 'once you start looking for them.'

'They're important,' George added, 'in the Gnostic Gospels too, where Mary Magdalen is portrayed as forever quarrelling with Peter. In the *Pistis Sophia* she goes so far as to complain that he "hates the female race".'

'So not much has changed,' Philip observed. 'As far as Rome is concerned.'

'The point is,' Faith resumed, 'that women seem to have enjoyed considerable freedom in the early Church. Even St.Paul's early letters celebrate their equality. It's only in Corinthians that the man is expected to command and the woman to be silent. Christianity was actually criticised by its enemies as a religion for women, Pliny, for example, expressing amazement that two slave-women were allowed to serve as ministers. They were probably deacons (like Phoebe in Romans 16). It's only later that they were edged out by the men, especially in the western Church. In the east they continued to serve as deacons until the eighth century at least.'

'So that's why you Anglicans have felt able to reintroduce women deacons,' Philip exclaimed.

George explained that Faith had a number of friends in the Ely diocese who were among the first women to be ordained deacons in the Church of England after the necessary legislation had been passed by the Synod in 1986. The fact that there was a well-documented tradition of women deacons in the early Church made it rather difficult for believers in tradition to oppose their re-introduction.

'Weren't these early women deacons somewhat limited in function?' asked Edward, who had remained respectfully silent for some time.

'That's what Roman Catholic ecclesiastical historians tend to argue,' replied George. 'The main function of these women deacons, they suggest, seems to have been to minister to other women, especially in baptism. Don't forget, in those days, baptism wasn't just a sprinkling with oil and water; it involved total immersion and being rubbed all over with oil.

'I can see that might have been a bit too exciting for some priests,' Philip commented.

Philip couldn't help conjuring up erotic images of early baptisms as he lay in bed that night. He also contemplated the distance Faith had travelled from their early days together. It was hard in some ways to connect the confident woman she had become with the timid young girl he had first met. Even her church seemed to be developing in ways he hadn't envisaged. Perhaps Newman was right, that it was impossible either for individuals or institutions to stay remain alive without changing. It was hard, however, to imagine his own Church even considering the possibility of ordaining women.

Chapter 9

Synod

The Church of England was clearly willing at least to consider change. Philip could remember vividly the excitement surrounding the final vote on the question of ordaining women as priests in the General Synod in November 1992. It had been a matter of vital concern for Faith, whose own future quite literally depended on the outcome. For when George had been appointed principal of a college in Durham earlier that year, she had given up her post in Cambridge in order to accompany him there. She had felt for some time a definite calling to the priesthood. Now, if the vote went through (for which it needed a two-thirds majority in all three houses of Synod) she intended to apply to one of the Durham theological colleges to begin her training as soon as possible. Philip, while finding the prospect of becoming the former boyfriend of a future priest a little alarming, was pleased that she and George had moved to Durham. It was only a brief walk from his office in New Elvet to the elegant Georgian house they had bought in Gilesgate. He remembered calling upon them there the evening before the vote in Synod to catch up on the latest developments.

'It's going to be very close,' Faith told him. 'The BBC has just released a poll predicting it will fail by one vote in the House of Laity. The other two houses should have clear majorities in favour of ordination but that one key vote could scupper everything. Then all hell would break loose.'

'Hell hath no fury...' began George. 'And the

number of women who would feel scorned by a "No" vote includes over a thousand women deacons. Faith seems to know half of them personally, if the number of phone calls we've received today is anything to go by.'

'The point is that if it doesn't go through tomorrow it may never do so,' Faith lamented. She was clearly very nervous about the outcome.

George outlined to Philip the long history of the debate within the Anglican Church. As long ago as 1978 the General Synod had decided that there were 'no fundamental objections' to the ordination of women. Deacons had been introduced in 1986 and a draft of the Priests (Ordination of Women) Measure passed in 1989. A positive outcome to this final vote would (with the approval of parliament) bring the Measure into force. The whole discussion had been dogged by controversy, especially when the American Episcopal Church jumped the gun by deciding unilaterally to ordain women.

'I suppose my own Church's opposition to the idea hasn't helped,' Philip ventured.

'No, it hasn't,' said Faith ruefully. 'One of the main reasons for the Anglo-Catholics opposing the Measure is the damage they think it will do to any prospects of unity with Rome. That was always a big concern for Archbishop Runcie. At least his successor is unambiguously in favour of women priests. George Carey even went so far as to call the idea that only a man can represent Christ "a most serious heresy".'

'That won't have gone down well in the Vatican,' Philip observed.

'It caused quite a stir here too,' George added. 'You wouldn't believe how political the Church of England has become. The elections for Synod in 1990 were as bitter as any General Election. There are so many factions fighting for their particular corner that it's hard to keep up with the acronyms. There's MOW (the Movement for the Ordination of Women), POW (Priests for the Ordination of Women) and even NOW (Newcastle Ordination of Women). I met a woman from this local organisation who showed me photographs of some of their demonstrations, including one with a woman with a dog bearing the sign, "Twelve years in the ministry but only the dog gets the collar".'

'There are some interesting placards outside Church House today,' Faith added. 'A black deacon has a sign saying "Women, Beautifully and Wonderfully Made in the Image of God".'

'That's one in the eye for St.Augustine,' Philip commented.

'It's also biblical,' added George; 'a reference to Psalm 139. She *is* beautiful too.'

'But we're *all* beautiful. That's the point.' Faith wasn't going to allow her husband's complete agreement with her on this issue to obscure the fact that he was a member of the privileged sex. Philip decided not to outstay his welcome and made his way to the station, promising to return the following day to catch the climax of the debate and the all-important vote.

'I'll bring some champagne in expectation of victory,' he announced.

'Or to drown our sorrows,' George cautioned.

It was about four o'clock the following afternoon when Philip returned to the house in Gilesgate to find the front room packed with excited women, watching the debate on television as it was broadcast live from Church House. He asked George how it had gone so far.

'As you'd expect. The debate has been running so long that there aren't any new arguments. Carey made quite an impressive speech this morning, firmly in favour. He said that God was calling us to take the risk of faith. The usual suspects have spoken against, painting a frightening picture of the chaos that will ensue if the Measure is passed, parish pitched against parish, diocese against diocese. Assorted conservative evangelicals have been quoting selected passages from St.Paul. Everyone's now waiting nervously for the vote. No-one's actually listening to the arguments.'

Philip saw that Faith had her eyes firmly glued to the screen. The television coverage kept cutting from the debate itself, which was dignified and restrained, if rather tense, to the more lively vigil outside in Dean's Yard, where supporters of women's ordination who were following the debate on the radio would occasionally burst into spontaneous applause and even from time to time into song. The cameras zoomed in on some of the more attractive women deacons, resplendent in their clerical gowns and collars. Inside the hall Dr.John Habgood, Archbishop of York, brought the debate to a close, calling for a brief period of prayer and reflection before they cast their votes. Then the members of Synod started to file through their respective doors, one for the Ayes and the other for the Noes.

'The moment of truth,' George announced as Dr.Carey stood up to announce the result, urging everyone to receive it with silence, whichever way it went. The House of Bishops and the House of Clergy, as expected, had passed the Measure with comfortable majorities, well over the two thirds required. All hinged on the House of Laity, which had voted 169 in favour, 82 against. There was a nervous silence while everyone did the necessary calculations and then a huge cheer arose from outside the hall as the supporters of women's ordination realised that they had won. But only just; two votes cast in the opposite direction would have seen the Measure fail.

Inside the hall, as requested, there was a dignified silence, although the television cameras focussed on women deacons hugging and weeping in the public gallery. Outside, supporters of women's ordination were dancing and cheering. Candles were lit, a stray firework flared into the evening sky and passing cars beeped their horns in solidarity. In Faith's front room too the women were hugging each other, alternately laughing and bursting into tears. Philip popped his bottle of champagne while George scurried around with glasses.

'To a brighter future,' he proposed.

'You realize that this is only the beginning,' Faith said.

'How do you mean?' Philip asked.

'The beginning of my new life,' she explained. 'It will take ages to train for the priesthood, even if I get accepted.'

She explained the long process of discernment through which all would-be ordinands had to go in order to assess whether she had a sufficiently robust faith and personality. This involved a series of interviews with members of the diocese, who would (if they thought fit) recommend her to the bishop sponsoring her training. She would then have to attend the Bishop's Selection Conference, a residential weekend involving more interviews, after which a final decision would be made. The training itself, for a graduate such as herself, would take two years before she could be ordained deacon. A year after that she could finally be ordained priest, though she would still need to serve a curacy of at least three years before she could become a vicar.

Philip was amazed. 'You mean all those vicars through whose sermons I dozed for years had gone through all this. No wonder they all seemed so tired!'

'It's the clerical life that does that to them,' George said. 'The perpetual round of baptisms, weddings and funerals, visiting the sick, trying to comfort those in hopeless situations, being perpetually kind to people. And don't think this is the end of the debate, either. Those who are opposed to women priests won't give in without a fight. They've already won some concessions included within the Measure itself, the financial compensation they can claim if they leave and the resolutions parishes can adopt if they don't want a woman serve as incumbent. And they'll ask for more, you can be sure of that.'

'How can they?' Philip asked. 'They've lost the vote; why don't they simply accept that and carry on, as people would in any other organisation.'

'That's not how the Church of England works,' Faith explained. 'We haven't got where we are today without centuries of infighting, fudge and compromise.'

'Or tolerance for different points of view,' her husband added, pouring her another drink.

As the champagne flowed, the mood of the people gathered in the house was becoming increasingly buoyant. If these scenes were repeated around the country, as they presumably were, then the Church of England was certainly getting an infusion of new blood, energy and hope. Faith and her friends spent the rest of the evening anticipating some of the changes the Synod vote would bring. After a few more drinks they began speculating on the date of the first female bishop and the first female Archbishop of Canterbury.

This initial euphoria was somewhat dented, however, in the immediate aftermath of the vote, when the Church of England found itself faced with threats of schism or mass desertion to Rome. Philip remembered hearing Faith complain over lunch about a year later that the Bishops seemed more concerned with keeping the disaffected traditionalists on board than with actually implementing the changes. They had hammered out an additional set of safeguards for those opposed to women priests, including the option for parishes not only not to have women incumbents themselves but to call upon the services of 'provincial episcopal visitors' or 'flying bishops' (as they were labelled in the press), if they were unhappy with their own bishop's support of women's ordination.

'It's as if those bishops were somehow tainted by such close association with women,' Faith complained. 'We should probably have made more of a fuss about these arrangements but we were still so pleased to have "won" that we let them through. Then the bishops began talking of a long "process of discernment" within the whole Church, as if the matter hadn't yet been resolved. The "two integrities", we were told, for and against women priests, needed to respect each other's positions. "Two integrities," my foot! It's more like two ferrets in a sack.'

Her disappointment at these developments was all too obvious, along with the ironic way in which she waggled her fingers at the bishops' phrases. Publicly, however, like other candidates for ordination, Faith had to be more circumspect, more tolerant of the different attitudes of others in her church. She herself had changed quite considerably over the years from the conservative evangelical background in which she had been reared to her current more liberal position.

'You've certainly come a long way since when we first met,' Philip commented.

'Well, I could hardly stay still.'

'Quite a few people seem to manage it.'

'Not really. So much changes in life that you can't

stay the same yourself. You have to adapt. Even the way I pray is different now, much less confident. It's more a form of meditation than a list of requests.'

'Well, I hope you don't develop that sing-song voice you hear in so many Anglican clerics. That always grates on my nerves.'

Faith's application to train for the priesthood had made good progress. She was going to attend her Bishop's Conference in the New Year and, all being well, begin her training in September.'

'So you've already had your private interview with the Bishop?'

'Yes,' Faith laughed. 'I think he's actually quite keen on me. He kept on putting his hand on mine, reassuringly, I suppose, but with just enough relish to be a little creepy. He's an enthusiastic supporter of women priests, of course, and spoke in most of the debates. When I mentioned some of the feminists I'd been reading, like Rosemary Radford Ruether, he leaped up, found copies of her books on his shelves, and started leafing through them. They were covered with marginal notes, so he'd obviously read them carefully. He also spoke excitedly about the first ordinations of women coming up next summer, coinciding with the fortieth anniversary of his own ordination.'

'It sounds as if you won't have much trouble from him then.'

'Not in the way of opposition, no. And I'm sure I can keep him at arm's length.'

Philip then launched into a critique of his own Church's response to the Anglican ordination of women, its preparedness to present itself as the last bastion of misogyny.

'Even Cardinal Hume, whom I normally respect, has said that the Catholic Church couldn't consider ordaining women. He said we didn't have the authority to make such a significant change. Lack of authority has hardly been a trait of the Catholic hierarchy in the past.'

'But you've not thought of returning to the Church of England?'

'I've thought about it, obviously. And I still do, every time our Church makes itself ridiculous (which is fairly often). But I still see the Catholic Church, for all its faults, as the universal church, historically and geographically. That's what the word "catholic" means.'

'Yes, Philip. I may not speak Latin and Greek but I am aware of that.'

'For me the Church of England seems too parochial, too closely rooted in one country. It's also too much part of the establishment, with the Queen as its Supreme Governor and the Prime Minister having the final say in episcopal appointments. At least the Catholic Church has a preferential option for the poor.'

'But it's so hierarchical. You have no democratic structures worthy of the name.'

'Well, we do now have parish pastoral councils at grass roots level even if these are only advisory. Mind you, we seem to have lost some of the momentum for change generated by the Second Vatican Council. I went to a series of seminars on Vatican Two in the Catholic Chaplaincy last month and couldn't help observing that most of the people who attended were clearly disappointed about recent developments. By the way, who do you think was at those seminars at Newcastle University?'

'I don't know, you tell me.'

'Rachel. She's now a member of her parish pastoral council. They have a new priest who is rather more liberal than the old one, which isn't difficult. She's left

Tony and is now living with her parents. I didn't know about all this because I've been attending the Cathedral since we separated.'

'So don't tell me, you've started seeing her again?'

'Yes I have, actually. We've met for a few drinks and I've even been to a couple of her concerts, just to show good will.'

Faith resisted the temptation to say she must be desperate. She already knew how desperate Philip himself had been. She could see that it would be a good thing for Philip if he and Rachel could get back together. Not that it would be easy; with Philip nothing ever was.

Chapter 10

Christmas

Philip's reconciliation with Rachel quickly became complete. After several lengthy conversations about the past, they decided to give their marriage a second chance. They also agreed, late though they had left it, that they still wanted to have children. Not before time, they both felt ready for the responsibility. So Rachel moved back into the terrace house in the West End of Newcastle, where they soon settled into a routine which involved spending more time together, talking things through more and showing more interest in each other's activities.

Faith too made progress, passing the Bishop's Selection Conference and being accepted to train for the priesthood at Cranmer Hall. The first ordinations of women had begun to take place, including that of thirty-eight women in Durham Cathedral at the end of May 1994. This coincided with Trinity Sunday, the fortieth anniversary of the Bishop's own ordination, and after the service the women gave him forty red roses, one for each year of his own ministry. Faith described the scene enthusiastically to Philip and Rachel over a meal in Newcastle that summer.

'It was such a positive event. After so much suffering and disappointment, so many years of waiting, these women were finally being recognised, released as it were from captivity. The way they flooded out of the Cathedral onto Palace Green after their ordination seemed symbolic of this liberation. It was like a wedding, only with thirty-eight brides.'

'Brides of Christ,' Philip couldn't resist commenting. 'Mind you, as in all marriages, there will presumably be difficulties.'

'They've already experienced some of these as deacons,' George added. 'You can't imagine the difficulty some people have in accepting women in dog collars. One of Faith's friends was mistaken for a kissogram when visiting a hospital ward. The lad she had come to visit, who had been hurt in a motorbike accident, fully expected her to start stripping off her vestments and dancing.'

'One of the problems our parishioners find,' Faith continued, 'is knowing what to call us. Some parishioners revert to their schooldays and call us "Miss". One of my friends, assigned to a High Church parish, was even addressed as "Father Mother". Older men, even when they mean to encourage us, can be very patronising. I was told by one old buffer, "You're far too pretty to be a priest". He meant it as a compliment, of course, but it was still rather annoying.'

'There must be more serious difficulties than that,' Philip observed. 'I've heard that there can be real hostility towards women priests.'

'It's normally fairly petty things, like refusing to take communion from a woman, or to shake hands at the kiss of peace. What normally happens is that anyone opposed to a woman curate in their church moves to a different parish. There's more of a problem when there are team ministries. They have to announce their rotas in advance so that people know if a woman is celebrating.'

'Doesn't that rather detract from the spirit of the whole thing?' Philip asked.

'Yes, but these are only temporary problems. I can't believe it will remain like this for long. People will have eventually to accept women priests or move on.'

'There's always the Catholic Church to fall back on,' Philip groaned.

'There haven't been that many conversions so far. Most people are staying put. Mind you, not that many women have actually been assigned to parishes yet. They reckon that there will be over a thousand women priests by the end of the year but there won't be enough posts to go round. Many will have to serve as non-stipendiary clergy to begin with, assisting in their own parishes. The situation is very uneven, varying from diocese to diocese according to the enthusiasm of the bishop.'

'Our bishop is very keen,' George admitted, 'especially on Faith.'

Faith blushed. 'He's really very sweet. It's just his manner that I find rather creepy. The only real hostility I've encountered is from other women. After all, they've been serving as unpaid curates for years. They presumably feel we are undermining their position.'

'That must be tricky,' Rachel acknowledged.

'Well, to be honest, it's all a bit tricky at the moment. We all feel under the microscope, our every move being watched in a way that male ordinands aren't. We have to prove that we can do the job well whereas many of them have been doing it badly for ages without anyone complaining. I sometimes feel that there's just not enough time in the day to do all that we're supposed to do. The assumption in the past has always been that the vicar himself won't have to worry about such mundane things as childcare, cooking, entertaining and so on, since his wife will do it for him. George does his share, of course, but he's not much of a wife.'

George pointed out that he did have a college to run. It was in the pause that followed that Rachel took the opportunity to break the news that she was expecting.

Faith and George expressed their delight but couldn't resist warning them of the ways in which their lives would change.

'I'd stock up on sleep now while you have the chance,' George warned.

Rachel and Philip were at least partly aware of what was in store for them. They were the oldest and most conscientious of the couples at their ante-natal classes, Philip in particular studying all the recommended books with great care. He knew that the other couples in the class found his studious approach to parenthood rather comic but that wasn't going to stop him making sure he did the best for his child. Rachel was more laid back about this as about everything else. The discovery that the child would be female sparked a long discussions of possible names.

'How about Eve?' Philip suggested.

'Definitely not. And do we have to have a biblical name?'

'Perhaps one of the more common ones, which won't stand out too much.'

In the end they settled on Sarah, a name sufficiently common not to draw attention to itself as biblical. Philip made sure that they had all the equipment they needed, including a beautiful wooden rocking cradle, complete with mobiles of animals, which they referred to as Noah's Ark. He also redecorated the small room they had earmarked for the child, developing a previously unsuspected talent for painting and wall-papering. As mid-December approached Rachel's blood pressure rose rather alarmingly, so she was taken into hospital, where the birth was finally induced. Philip insisted on being present throughout the labour although his excitement became so irritating that the midwife threatened to give him an epidural if he didn't calm down. When young Sarah finally arrived, bawling her heart out, she was quickly wrapped in a shawl and placed in Philip's arms. He then brought her to Rachel and the two of them cradled the little child, who lay there quietly, turning from one to the other as if not quite sure what to make of them.

That Christmas was unlike any other that Philip had experienced. All the stories at which he had previously scoffed began to acquire new meaning. Hearing Rachel's choir sing the familiar words, 'Unto us a child is born', he could now share fully in the celebration of the gift of life. Contemplating the nativity scene in church, the infant Jesus surrounded not just by his parents but by oxen, sheep and asses, it seemed entirely appropriate that all life should be represented. He didn't even complain about the angels, so long as they were understood as symbolic. He had never, of course, underestimated the importance of the wise men. His new-found joy, his relish for all the trappings of Christmas and babyhood did not go unnoticed.

'He seems like a different person,' Rachel's mother confided to her one day.

'He not only seems like one; he is,' came the reply. 'I don't think anything has taken him out of himself like this before, not even when we first met. I suppose it's the fact of being entirely responsible for the welfare of this small creature.'

Philip threw himself into all aspects of fatherhood, from late night feeding (after Sarah was weaned off the breast) to nappy-changing. He would laugh when Sarah lay back on her mat, wriggling and kicking in resistance to all her father's attempts to fasten her nappy. When this process was finally complete, he would cradle her in his arms, rocking her from side to side and singing songs that he had forgotten that he knew, songs that had been sung to him as a child. He pushed her proudly through the streets in her pram, parading her to the neighbours. Even in the department, when he resumed work, he treated his colleagues to endless stories of her infant wisdom and precocity. And when she started talking Philip recorded each new word in a notebook, a permanent reminder of the astonishing process of language acquisition. Rachel joked that the child had become his latest research project but she was pleasantly surprised at the warmth of his affection for her.

The three of them started attending the Catholic Chaplaincy at Newcastle University, a hollowed-out terrace house which was rather more child-friendly than their local church. The space in which Mass was celebrated was comfortably carpeted, allowing babies and toddlers to roam freely around the room with little danger of hurting themselves. The chaplaincy was primarily intended for students but had attracted a number of young members of staff (and some not so young) who found the informality of the proceedings and the more liberal theology more to their taste than their own parishes. Philip had a number of nicknames for them, 'children of the sixties', 'ageing hippies' and 'refugees from suburbia'. But he recognised in them some of his own rebellious qualities.

Philip and his fellow-refugees found themselves very much in sympathy with a new movement of radical Catholics, entitled 'We Are Church'. Founded in Austria and Germany in 1995, it had quickly spread to other countries, including the United Kingdom, which sent delegates to a conference in Rome the following November. There they produced a document entitled 'The Roman Petition' calling for a number of reforms to the Catholic Church, particularly in the areas of gender and sexuality. The priesthood, they demanded, should be open to both men and women, married and celibate. The whole message of the Church should be much more positive, a matter of joy not threat, of celebration not denial. The laity should be consulted much more widely, especially in the area of sexuality, where their experience was clearly greater than that of the clergy.

One of the delegates to the conference in Rome, a lecturer in the Department of Religious Studies, whom Philip had met at the cathedral, arranged a meeting at the chaplaincy at Newcastle to discuss 'The Roman Petition'. Philip and Rachel, eager to learn more about the movement (and to have an evening out of the house), attended the first of these on a bitterly cold evening in December 1996, leaving the two-year-old Sarah in the capable hands of Rachel's mother. It began with a brief introduction explaining that the movement had arisen out of widespread disappointment at the Church's failure fully to embrace Vatican Two. When the meeting was opened to the floor it became increasingly obvious how widespread dissatisfaction among the audience with the Church as it was. What was less clear was whether there was sufficient agreement about the reforms necessary to put things right. It was decided to reconvene in January in an attempt to agree on a few practical suggestions for reform on which they could focus.

That meeting in the New Year decided to focus on sexual questions, challenging the official teaching of the Church on contraception and homosexuality in particular. Many of the people who attended were also concerned about the Church's handling of some recent cases widely reported in the media of alleged sexual abuse of children by priests. There seemed to have been at least one case in their own diocese of a priest against whom there had been serious allegations of abuse simply being moved to another parish. The lack of openness about the whole procedure had been difficult to excuse. It was particularly galling that Catholics who were responsible neither for the policies nor the abuse should have to share in the shame.

The discussion became heated as several contributors attempted to establish a link between the requirement of celibacy and such incidents of child abuse. It was impossible to prove, of course, but the increasing number of scandals now emerging in the Catholic Church across the world suggested at least some connection between the two. Living in an increasingly sexualised world, priests seemed to be finding their repressed sexuality returning to haunt them, sometimes in extreme and perverse forms. The hierarchy maintained that it was simply a matter of a few 'rotten apples' who could be removed by more careful screening of applicants to the priesthood. But the cloak of secrecy with which the whole subject had been sealed was only symptomatic of the Church's attitude to sexuality in general.

Unusually for him, Philip contributed little to the discussion. Because of his own experience of all-male institutions, he was able to speak a little about the warping of emotions they could cause. But he spoke in general terms only; to voice such private matters in public was something he still found difficult. He decided not to stand for the committee which was elected at the meeting. The abuse he had suffered, he explained to Rachel afterwards, had not been a result of specifically Catholic institutions.

'Are you saying that there is a specifically Catholic form of sexual abuse?' she asked.

'Yes, I suppose I am. Sexual abuse of children is a universal phenomenon, of course, but the requirement of celibacy is peculiar to the Catholic Church. The formation of priests and the unbridled power they enjoy in their own parishes is also particular to the Catholic

Church. These are specific conditions that serve to foster such abuse.'

'So why weren't you willing to address them yourself by standing for the committee?'

'Because my own background and experience isn't Catholic. I was messed up by entirely secular institutions. And because I'm so messed up I don't feel confident about offering solutions. What kind of expertise could I offer?'

'That's never held you back in the past,' Rachel laughed.

'No, but I'm beginning to learn my limitations. Besides, I don't want to be in a perpetual rage with the Church.'

'I thought you were, anyway.'

'Not all the time.'

Philip explained that he had resolved to be less critical of everyone and everything (including the Church), to be more positive in outlook. He had recently been approached in connection with some planned celebrations of the Millennium in Durham in a few years' time: "Two Thousand years of Christian Heritage". It had been suggested that he might write something for the occasion and he thought of attempting a modern mystery play. He was currently mulling over the possibilities.

Chapter 11

Millennium

Philip's resolve to be more positive about everything was severely tested in the next few years as the rigours of parenting took their toll. Constant sleep deprivation, as George had warned, left him feeling perpetually tired. So severe were his complaints about the way Sarah kept him up at night and woke him early in the morning that he became known by some of his less sympathetic colleagues in the department as a walking advertisement for contraception.

'It's easier dealing with children when you're younger,' Faith told him when both couples met for a drink in Newcastle shortly after Sarah's fourth birthday party, the strains and stresses of which Philip recounted in all their gory detail. They had hired a room with a bouncing castle in a local leisure centre. Philip had never seen such a mass of writhing limbs going in all directions and had been convinced one of the children would be seriously hurt. The meal which followed, he insisted, made the feeding of the five thousand seem like a picnic.

'I seem to find everything twice as difficult as it used to be. I'm struggling at the moment to make sense of what used to seem straightforward. For instance, for my Millennium Passion Play I'm trying to construct a coherent character for Judas but the more I think about it, the more confused I get.'

'Isn't he just your conventional villain, the baddie of the story?' Faith suggested.

'Well, that's what he becomes in the tradition. But

there are hints in the gospels that he must have had some good qualities or he wouldn't have been chosen as one of the twelve in the first place, certainly not entrusted with the finances. I know he's supposed to have embezzled money from them, according to John at least, but why did Jesus choose him in the first place? It seems to show a lack of judgment.'

'Wasn't Judas deliberately chosen to be the traitor, the one who would betray him?' Faith asked. 'Doesn't Jesus actually say, "One of you is a devil" at the end of that chapter of John?'

'But isn't that too simple?' Philip objected. 'Making him a satanic figure. It also deprives him of any choice, condemning him to evil and guilt for the sake of the plot.'

'But that's what John suggests: "The devil had already planted it in the heart of Judas...to betray him." Then Jesus makes it clear that the one to whom he gives the piece of bread will be the one to betray him.'

'There's an *Arabic Infancy Gospel* of the fifth or sixth century,' George added, 'which has the young Judas try to bite the young Jesus because he's possessed by Satan. If I remember rightly, Satan then assumes the shape of a mad dog and runs away.'

'That would hardly work on stage. And besides, I want something a bit more plausible than that, a bit more realistic in terms of modern psychology. Why, for example, does Jesus tell him, "Do quickly what you are going to do." The other disciples clearly don't understand what Judas is being told to do. As far as they're concerned he might just have been given instructions about the shopping . But there seems to be a definite understanding between Judas and Jesus that this "handing over" to the Jews has to be done. Judas is actually serving Jesus in this. And yet he comes to such a sticky end, hanging himself, according to Matthew, and "bursting asunder" at the beginning of the Acts of the Apostles. Papias claims that he grew so fat that he couldn't see and that he peed pus and worms. The Gnostic gospels paint a much more sympathetic portrait of him. In the *Gospel of Judas*, for example he's the only one who understands who Jesus is and why he must be handed over to be crucified.'

'I've never heard of the *Gospel of Judas*,' Rachel confessed.

'Well, it was only dug out of the ground in the 1970s,' George explained. 'And then it was locked in a safe-deposit box on Long Island for ages. It still hasn't been published. Irenaeus refers to it at the end of the second century so it must have been written before then. It presents Jesus thanking Judas for releasing him from his body, for handing him over to be crucified so that he can finally return to God. Judas also features prominently in another second-century Gnostic text discovered at Nag Hammadi, *The Dialogue of the Saviour*, which presents him as an inquirer after the truth who learns from Jesus that the Kingdom of Heaven is to be found within.'

'So which is the real Judas?' Philip asked, a note of desperation creeping into his voice. 'The traitor of the canonical gospels or the Gnostic visionary?'

'What he actually does is the same in all versions,' George answered. 'They only differ over his motives. And for at least some of those the canonical gospels turned to the Old Testament: the thirty pieces of silver, for example.'

'The most convincing portrait of Judas I've come across so far,' Philip continued, 'is that of Dorothy Sayers in *The Man Born to Be King*. She sees him as the most intelligent of the disciples, the only one to grasp the necessity of the crucifixion. He's a passionate idealist who projects his own ideals onto Jesus and resents it when some of the other disciples are preferred to him.'

'That's psychologically convincing anyway,' Rachel admitted.

'I suppose I have *carte blanche* to write what I like,' Philip admitted. 'But I want so much to get at the *truth,* to show what *really* happened. It's hard to settle for just another plausible interpretation. The other character who is keeping me awake at night (apart from Sarah) is Mary Magdalen.'

'Why am I not surprised by that?' Faith ventured wearily.

'No, seriously. There's such a difference between the traditional notion of her as the penitent sinner, the reformed prostitute, and what's actually in the gospels, both canonical and apocryphal. There's nothing in any of them about her being a prostitute.'

'No,' George confirmed. 'That only came about by conflating her with the sinner in Luke 7 who anointed Jesus's feet with precious ointment and the woman caught in adultery in John 8. You can blame Pope Gregory the Great for deciding that all these women were actually Mary Magdalen.'

'It certainly makes for a great story,' Rachel said. 'The tart with the heart who is forgiven because she showed such great love.'

'There's no evidence for her being a tart,' George insisted, 'but there are hints in some of the Gnostic gospels that she might have been especially close to Jesus. The *Gospel of Philip* refers to her as Jesus's partner or consort. It's in that gospel that he is said to kiss her. She is the only woman to get her own gospel, the *Gospel of Mary*, in which she takes a leading role, consoling the other disciples after the crucifixion and revealing to them what Jesus taught her in private.'

'Even in the canonical gospels Mary Magdalen

plays a very significant role,' Faith insisted. 'She stays with Jesus through everything, which is more than Peter does, and then she's chosen as a prime witness to the resurrection. That scene in John where Jesus tells her not to touch him is interesting because it implies that their relationship *was* normally physical.'

'So what do I do?' Philip asked. 'Do I go with the traditional penitent sinner or with the Saviour's favourite companion?'

'I'd go with Gregory the Great and conflate them,' George suggested. 'It makes for a better story.'

'That's what people want,' Rachel agreed. 'A good story, one where they can identify with the characters. That's why Mary Magdalen has proved so popular. It gives us all hope to think that whatever we may have done, we can be forgiven.'

'But it's not as if I'm writing fiction; I'm trying to get at the truth about Jesus and his disciples. You can see that, can't you Faith?'

'If I were you,' Faith replied, 'I'd make her a feminist. That has a certain topicality to it.'

'I don't know,' Philip stammered, still far from happy. 'None of you seem to care for the truth; all you're interested in is the effect on the audience.'

'Isn't that the most important thing about the Bible?' Faith asked. 'That's why people continue to read it, because it helps them, comforts them, inspires them even.'

'Even if it isn't true?' Philip asked.

'If there's one thing I have learnt from the churches in which I've been placed so far,' Faith said, 'it's that people don't come there to learn about history.'

'What do they come for then?' Philip asked.

'All sorts of things,' Faith answered. 'Company, for a start. Many of the older people at my current church don't have many friends, don't see anyone at all some days. It gives them comfort to be part of a larger community.'

'They could go to a Bingo Hall for that,' Philip snapped.

'Maybe. But our community has a more dignified story to tell, a set of stories, in fact, which help people to live fuller lives, to care about others, to see some overall purpose to everything.'

'So that's it, then,' Philip snorted, 'the revelation that Christianity has to offer, the good news as currently preached by the Church of England?'

'No, of course not,' Faith responded, somewhat taken aback by his vehemence. 'You asked me why people came to church and I was attempting to put an answer together.'

'You'll have to forgive him,' Rachel intervened. 'It's the lack of sleep that makes him so irritable.'

Philip also apologised for his rudeness and the four of them continued their meal more peacefully, carefully avoiding the subject of religion. On their way home, however, Rachel asked Philip how he could have been so aggressive towards such a good friend as Faith, especially on a question so close to her new vocation. Philip himself found it hard to explain where his anger had come from.

'I suppose all this study of the gospels has brought home all those problems raised by Strauss about their historicity.'

'Well, you should try to keep them to yourself. The last thing Faith needs right now is someone questioning the historical basis of her beliefs.'

'I know. I'm sorry for being such a boar.'

'Is that boar or bore?' Rachel asked.

Philip laughed and the tension between them was partially diffused. When they reached home, Sarah made them laugh even more, explaining how naughty her babysitter had been.

'She wouldn't let me watch my video and said I had to go to bed. Then she watched a video of her own full of naked men.'

'It was only *A Room with a View*,' the babysitter explained, blushing. 'It has a U certificate but there's a scene where three of the male characters, including the vicar, romp around the lake without their clothes. Sarah came down and saw it because she heard me laughing.'

Sarah was reassured that nakedness was all right – that it was nothing to be ashamed of – and quickly went back to sleep. Philip resumed work on his Passion Play, which began to take shape, with Judas as a disillusioned intellectual and Mary Magdalen as a passionate feminist. He enjoyed putting some of his own intensity into the character of Judas and giving Mary Magdalen a combination of Rachel's sensuality and Faith's convictions.

One by-product of this project was an invitation to talk about it to an organisation of which he and Rachel had only recently become aware: Catholic People's Weeks. Described by a friend as a cross between a week at Butlin's and a retreat, it involved Catholic families descending on some unsuspecting boarding school for a week during the summer holidays. There was a programme of lectures and seminars for the adults, normally focussed on a religious theme, and a separate programme for children, led by teenagers. The idea was to foster a more thinking and active laity at the same time as providing hard-pressed parents with some relief during school holidays. Founded by some well-meaning Catholic academics in the 1950s, it had gained momentum after the Second Vatican Council as a means of educating the laity for the increased responsibility they were now expected to bear.

The theme of the week to which Philip and Rachel

were invited was the role of the arts in the Church. Rachel was going to talk about Verdi's Requiem and Philip about the Medieval Mystery Plays. The boarding school at which this particular week was being held boasted an outdoor swimming pool and tennis courts among its amenities. The food and accommodation were rather Spartan, reminding Philip of his schooldays. But the camaraderie was evident; everyone introduced themselves and welcomed the 'newcomers' warmly. There was a daily Mass, celebrated by the resident priest, Father Thomas, a university chaplain who was clearly at home with the informality of the proceedings. There was also a bar every evening, run by members of the group on a rota basis, which helped even Philip to relax. There were plenty of children of Sarah's age with whom she quickly made friends.

The opening talk involved an archaeologist showing slides of early Christian representations of Jesus, including a mosaic of a beardless Christ from a fourth-century villa in Dorset, well before Christianity was officially introduced into the country. Philip found it fascinating to see the changing face of Christ as imagined by artists from different times and cultures, to trace a growing realism as the Byzantine celebration of the triumphant Christ on the cross gave way to the medieval Man of Sorrows. This anticipated some of the themes in Philip's own talk the following morning, which focussed on the increasingly elaborate liturgical celebrations of the medieval period. Tenth-century Easter services, for example, had included the acting out of the visit to the sepulchre by the three Maries. This in turn developed into a particular kind of drama, the 'Quem Quaritis?' (Whom do you seek?) based on the question posed to the women by the angel at the tomb of the risen Christ. These short plays became increasingly elaborate, some versions developing scenes from Mary Magdalen's earlier life as a sinner, showing her buying cosmetics and even soliciting men. She soon repented, of course, but the impulse to represent her as a convincing character could be tracked through these early attempts at drama.

Philip proceeded to recount some of the difficulties he had faced in writing his own Passion Play, in particular over the characterisation of Judas and Mary Magdalen. One point that he tried to emphasise, however, was that it was difficult to decide at what point liturgy turned into drama. He insisted that there had always been a theatrical dimension to the Mass, which involved a 'staging' of the Last Supper. He also argued that changes made at Vatican II in the position of the celebrant, no longer facing away from the congregation but towards them, reflected significant changes in our understanding of God. He was no longer seen as an object located 'out there' but a shared image constructed from within.

'You mean that He doesn't actually exist?' asked an elderly man at the back of the hall.

'No, I mean that our image of Him is the closest we can get to what is ultimately mysterious, beyond our intellectual grasp.'

'So we can't know Him?'

'Not in the way that we know other objects, no. We only catch glimpses of His existence at best. And I say "His" although He shouldn't really be thought of as gendered. It's just that we can't imagine a person without a gender. Not that He's a person either in the normal sense of the word. In attempting to represent what we can never fully know we're necessarily reduced to metaphors drawn from what we do know.'

Philip realised that he was cutting a rather comic figure as a 'typical' academic, incapable of certainty about anything. The questioner began muttering about intellectuals disappearing up their own backsides but made way for other people to raise other issues. These included a particularly complex question about 'real presence' and transubstantiation, to which Philip gave an even less convincing answer. He tried to explain that we no longer thought in terms of a binary opposition between substance and accidence, inner reality and external form. He defended a notion of sacramentality, that things could partake of as well as point towards a deeper reality not fully understood. But he distrusted anyone who talked confidently about 'being' and 'presence'. Fortunately Father Thomas came to his rescue at this point, giving a brief historical explanation of how transubstantiation had come to be defined at the Fourth Lateran Council in 1215.

Rachel's talk, later that same day, went down rather better than Philip's. She was so familiar with Verdi and his career that she was able to present it entirely without notes. She illustrated her talk with several excerpts from the Requiem, some of which she sang herself. In the bar that night it became clear whose presentation most people had preferred. Father Thomas, however, made a point of telling Philip how much he had enjoyed his talk. Philip in turn thanked him for coming to his rescue over transubstantiation.

'It's not a word much used these days,' Father Thomas acknowledged. 'It's reduced to a footnote in the recent ARCIC document on the Eucharist.'

Philip, who had followed the proceedings of the Anglican Roman Catholic International Commission with a very personal interest, nodded agreement. He could see that he would need an influential ally in order to survive the week. But he surprised himself by enjoying the remaining days much more than he had anticipated. He was even allowed to read some of his poems, including one about Swedish altar girls, who had apparently been banned for distracting members of the congregation.

He returned to Durham with renewed energy and enthusiasm, completing the script of his Passion Play in time for rehearsals to start well in advance of the production, which was scheduled for the last few days 1999. He had to alter some of the dialogue during rehearsal, the actress playing the part of Mary Magdalen, for example, insisting on sexing up the role. It was all very well for first-wave feminists to play down their sexuality, she insisted, but she was damned if she was going to appear in jeans. Judas too objected to some of his more complex utterances, which were duly simplified. But Philip remained firm in the face of complaints by some of the other disciples about their portrayal as uncomprehending fools. They were told to take another look at themselves (as they were portrayed in the gospels). The final version of the play, while differing considerably from what Philip had first written , went down well with its audience, who were, of course, predisposed to be sympathetic. The Anglican Bishop, who embarrassed Faith by sitting next to her and whispering comments in her ear throughout the performance, was particularly pleased. The Catholic Bishop fell asleep halfway through but this didn't prevent him from lavishing praise on the whole production. Philip's credit within church circles rose significantly.

Chapter 12

Priest

Philip entered the new millennium full of good resolutions. He promised Rachel that he would be particularly supportive of Faith in her new position as curate of St.Oswald's in Durham, a church within walking distance of her house attended by a mixed congregation of students and local people. It had a strong musical tradition, including a children's choir, with which she was well equipped to help. Philip went to hear them sing and her preach on several occasions. He had at first found this strange but she had a clear, straightforward style which he quickly came to appreciate. She would always place the biblical text in context, explaining as clearly as possible what it would have meant to its original audience. She would then proceed to bring out its relevance for their own lives in the present.

The congregation loved her. In comparison to some of the more pompous male clergy they had endured, she brought a breath of fresh air, a genuine modesty about herself combined with a real interest in each of the parishioners. She was so assiduous in visiting the sick and housebound that George complained that he hardly ever saw her. He also warned her that she was in danger of wearing herself out. But there was little sign of this that anyone else noticed. She was clearly in her element, throwing herself wholeheartedly into her new role.

Philip found it more difficult to be positive about his own local church, to which he and Rachel had returned once Sarah started attending the primary school with which it had close links. They had begun to feel a bit out of place among the enthusiastic guitar-strumming students who attended the university Catholic chaplaincy. Behaving like an adolescent was difficult to maintain once you hit the age of fifty, Philip explained to the university chaplain when they made the decision. The main problem with their local parish was the new priest, Father James, to whom Philip took an instant dislike. Still relatively young, probably in his late thirties, he had one of those soft clerical voices and an ingratiating manner which set Philip's teeth on edge. He also had long black hair, which was always beautifully groomed.

'You're just jealous that he's got more hair than you,' Rachel told him when he confided his dislike to her.

'It's not that,' Philip insisted. 'There's something about him that I don't trust. I dislike the way he interacts with children in particular.'

'I think you're being paranoid,' Rachel argued. 'At least give the man a chance.'

Philip let the matter drop, for the time being at least. It was only when Sarah expressed interest in becoming an altar server that the prospect of putting his own child in the care of Father James reawakened his concerns. Sarah was now eight and had inherited some of the best features of both her parents. She was an open, trusting child, eager to please. Philip sometimes wished she were more critical and suspicious. Obedience, he would say, was a somewhat over-rated virtue in the Catholic Church. He couldn't quite bring himself to say what he actually thought ('Don't let that smarmy priest get his hands on you') but he did encourage Sarah to be wary of any adult being too friendly with her.

'How can anyone be too friendly?' Sarah asked.

'Well, it's not unknown for adults to befriend children for the wrong reasons,' Philip replied. 'Sometimes they want to do unpleasant things to you. If that ever happens, you must be sure to let us know.'

Sarah looked puzzled while Rachel, who had overheard most of the conversation from the kitchen, laughed out loud: 'For God's sake stop pussyfooting around. If you have grounds for suspicion you should make a complaint. If not, keep your thoughts to yourself.'

Philip remained unhappy, however, about the prospect of Sarah coming into closer contact with Father James and resolved to consult some of the other parents whose children were already serving on the altar. He also decided to read the Nolan Report, with its recommended procedures to protect children from abuse.

'It's really quite good,' he told Rachel after reading it. 'Like all committee reports, it's rather repetitive: it tells you what it was set up to do, then does it, then tells you what it's done. But it offers a number of practical recommendations. Mind you, I don't think they've been as widely publicised within the parish as they might have been. Did you know, for example that we are now supposed to have a Parish Child Protection Officer?'

'Yes, it's Martin Smith,' Rachel replied. 'His name appears on the back of the bulletin every week under CRB (Criminal Records Bureau). Anyone who works with children has to be checked by the police to make sure that they don't have a criminal record.'

'Isn't that rather hidden away under those initials on the back of a bulletin no one reads.'

'You may not read it, Philip, or know anything about working with children, but other people do.'

'Okay, so I live in an ivory tower but I do look out of its windows every now and then. And there are so many of these acronyms that it's quite difficult to keep up with them all. There's another thing I noticed in the report. Most abusers, it says, are men who suffer from loneliness and find it hard to make close relationships with adults. Who does that remind you of?'

'Don't tell me. Father James?'

'Quite a number of priests, in fact. The requirements of the priesthood seem almost designed to produce lonely and isolated men. The report suggests that more care be taken over the selection of priests but makes no comment whatsoever about the requirement of celibacy.'

'It probably wasn't in their remit.'

'But don't you think it should have been? Most of the publicity has been about the handling of cases of abuse by priests, the failure of bishops to alert the statutory authorities. But that's not the cause of the problem.'

'There's not much you can do about human nature, hun.'

'But that's precisely what the Church claims, that grace can help us overcome nature. So we have all these rules about celibacy and so on, only for nature to fight back. Those natural instincts we try to repress won't go away; they come back in distorted forms.'

'You should know, hun.'

'That's precisely it; I do know. I was brought up in some of the least healthy institutions in the world and then chose to join one that had managed to find a way of being even less healthy.'

'Put like that, pet, it doesn't sound good. So what are you planning to do about it?'

'Well, one good element in the Nolan Report is its encouragement of "whistle blowers", people who report their suspicions about a particular person to the diocesan Child Protection Co-ordinator. It can be an actual disclosure, an allegation about an act of abuse, or it can simply be a suspicion that someone is behaving inappropriately, seeing children on their own when it could be avoided. There's also an Annex which gives some simple rules about how adults should behave with children, avoiding inappropriate contact, for example, or favouritism.'

'What a brave new world we now live in,' Rachel moaned.

'It's a shame, I know. But when it comes to protecting children, as the report says, we need what they call "a culture of vigilance".'

'And I can see who has appointed himself Vigilante in Chief.'

Philip refused to be deterred by Rachel's mockery and continued making discreet enquiries among other parents of altar servers. This wasn't altogether easy. He could hardly go up to people he didn't know and ask if they thought the priest was interfering with their child. But he asked as much as he could about the training the altar servers received. Many of the parents didn't seem to know (or care) much about it. They just thought their children looked cute in their white robes; it hadn't struck them that the priest might think so too. Father James, however, as far as Philip could see, followed all the recommended procedures; he never saw individual altar servers on their own, for example, but always in groups. Philip therefore agreed to Sarah becoming an altar server although he insisted on her reporting everything that Father James did and said.

'You're turning her into some kind of spy or informer,' Rachel complained.

'That's better than becoming a victim of abuse.'

'Maybe. But you're in danger of investing her with all your own neuroses.'

'We do that anyway. "They fuck you up, your Mum

and Dad",' he began intoning before Rachel hushed him up.

Sarah was quite surprised that her father was taking such an interest in this particular aspect of her life; he didn't ask nearly so many questions about her life at school. And some of the questions seemed a bit odd. Why should he care so much whether Father James was nice to them?

'Of course, he's nice, Dad. He's a priest; he's supposed to be nice to people.'

'In what ways is he nice?' Philip persisted.

'I don't know. He smiles at us, encourages us, praises us when we do things properly.'

'Does he give you things? Presents or anything.'

'Not normally. I think we're going to get medals when we've been altar servers for a year.'

'So he never gives you sweets or anything?'

'He gave us all a piece of chocolate the other day. Is that the sort of thing you mean?'

'For God's sake,' Rachel intervened, 'give it a rest. You sound like the Spanish Inquisition.'

In the event it was not Philip's amateur sleuthing which brought about Father James's unmasking but someone working on the parish bulletin who noticed something suspicious on the priest's personal computer. He reported it to the police who found evidence of child pornography. Father James was duly suspended pending further investigation, causing much dismay (and gossip) in the parish.

'You needn't look so pleased with yourself,' Rachel told Philip when he told her the news.

'I'm not pleased. I find it very sad, both for him personally and for the Church. I'm relieved, of course, that Sarah has escaped his clutches. But I'm also annoyed that everyone seems to be putting all the blame on Father James as if it's just him that's rotten.'

'Who do you expect them to blame? In the end it's the individual who's responsible for his actions.'

'Precisely: in the *end*. But there are so many other factors involved. The whole way in which the Church treats sexuality needs overhauling.'

'Since when did you become an expert on sex?' Rachel scoffed.

'It's not up to me,' Philip objected. 'It's up to the Church as a whole, including the laity. It's the insistence that all decisions should to be in the hands of a group of celibate old men that helped to create the problem in the first place.'

'So what do you suggest: compulsory sex education for bishops?'

'That might be a start. Seriously, we have to do something.'

Some of Philip's concerns were shared by the Parish Pastoral Council, who requested a meeting with the bishop to discuss the issue. Bishop Andrew was a much-loved and highly respected man, who had been the abbot of a Benedictine monastery before reluctantly accepting the call to become a bishop. He was a gentle man, not one to enjoy laying down the law. He agreed to attend an open meeting in the church hall at which people could express their views.

'That's brave of him,' Philip commented. 'It could become quite nasty.'

'I don't think so,' Rachel replied. 'People genuinely love him. They won't blame him personally for this.'

The atmosphere in the hall prior to the meeting was certainly lively. The buzz of conversation only began to quieten when the bishop entered the building, accompanied by a few priests from the deanery and the diocesan Child Protection Co-ordinator, who explained the action that had been taken with regard to Father James. She was a relatively young childcare professional with a brisk, business-like manner, and restricted herself to the facts of the case, leaving the bishop to raise some of the broader questions. It was a terrible scandal, he acknowledged, that the Church, which sought to set the highest standards, to be a light to the world, should find itself mired in cases such as this. He urged anyone who had suffered any abuse from Father James or from any other priest to report it in confidence. Professional help would be made available to any victims who wanted it. Meanwhile the purpose of the meeting was to hear more general suggestions people might have about the way the Church could prevent similar cases arising.

There were, as might have been expected, a number of questions about the selection and training of priests. One man asked why it was possible for married Anglican clergy who converted to Rome to serve as Catholic priests while existing priests weren't permitted to marry. Bishop Andrew admitted that this seemed unfair and inconsistent. There was a difference, he insisted, between these special cases and the general expectation of celibacy, which enabled priests to devote themselves entirely to the needs of their parishes. Besides, he added, the Church would have to be prepared to pay much higher salaries to its clergy to enable them all to support families.

Philip wanted to press Bishop Andrew more closely on the question of celibacy. But he knew the way most cradle Catholics thought about their faith as something handed down from generation to generation, an unchanging 'deposit of faith' which it was not for them to question. Directly to challenge any aspect of Church teaching smacked to many of them of disloyalty. Philip had tried invoking the parable of the talents to suggest that they were in danger of burying the treasure of faith, quite literally depositing it in the ground rather than allowing it to grow. But it was difficult to refute the objection that was always made: he had chosen to join their church, and if he didn't like it, he could choose to leave.

He began seriously to consider rejoining the Church of England, especially after he and Rachel attended Faith's induction as vicar of the church of St.Andrew with St.Anne in Bishop Auckland. St.Andrew's was a large medieval church in the southern part of the town, more like a cathedral than a church, and it was linked with St.Anne's, a small church in the market place. It was quite a responsibility for her to have been offered this particular living, right under the nose of the bishop, who lived in the castle nearby. The fact that some Anglican bishops still lived in castles, Philip reminded himself, was one of the things he disliked about the established church.

The service of induction, however, he found very moving. It involved a whole series of solemn oaths and declarations on Faith's part, which she delivered with a clear, unfaltering voice. The bishop then read the formal document of institution, with Faith kneeling humbly before him. He said a prayer of blessing, bestowing upon her 'the cure of souls' within the parish. She rose gracefully (not that easy in a heavy black cassock) and accompanied him and the churchwardens to the main door of the church where he formally inducted her into the possession of the parish. A churchwarden then gave her the keys of the parish.

'Just like St.Peter,' Philip whispered.

The most moving part of the service, however, for Philip at least, came after this, when Faith pronounced what it meant to be a servant of Christ:

'We are to bring good news to the poor, to proclaim liberty to the captives and recovery of sight to the blind, to set free the oppressed and to announce that the time has come when the Lord will save his people. We are to make new disciples of Christ, to build up one another in the faith, and celebrate the sacraments of the new covenant.'

The ceremony continued with Faith being presented with a Bible, to symbolise her teaching, a bowl of water, representing her duty to baptise, a chalice and paten, representing the sacraments, and a service book, signifying worship. All this led into the Eucharistic celebration in which both Rachel and Philip joined, as Faith had said they should even though it wasn't strictly permitted by their own church.

'That's what being a priest is about,' Philip told Rachel afterwards over a glass of wine in the church hall. 'Preaching, baptising, celebrating the sacraments and worship. You don't have to be a man to do that, or celibate.'

'Okay,' she replied. 'There's no need for you to preach. Faith is supposed to do that.'

'It's just so frustrating. We have such a shortage of priests in the Catholic Church and they go on postponing the obvious remedy. When will they ever realise?'

'Maybe they will eventually.'

'I only hope you're right. I wish I had faith.'

'There she is,' Rachel laughed. 'I know you've always wanted her.'

Faith was indeed approaching them, smiling as ever, clearly relieved that the service itself was over and that she hadn't tripped over her cassock or disgraced herself in any other way. Rachel told her that she had a potential convert in Philip, who had been drooling over her throughout the service.

'Not exactly drooling,' Philip insisted, 'but I did enjoy the service. I still have a great deal of affection for the Anglican Church.'

He had seriously considered leaving the Catholic Church, whose leaders seemed to reject all calls for change. The characteristic response of the Vatican to criticism was to discipline those from whom it came, at least if they were subject to their control (as priests and religious were). If they were laity, of course, they could simply be ignored. And yet, however angry he often felt with the hierarchy of his Church, it was still the place where he felt most at home. As he joined the motley collection who shuffled forward to receive communion every Sunday, rich and poor, male and female, white and black, all of them reaffirming their corporate identity as the body of Christ, any residual anger disappeared. He was part of this family, dysfunctional as it might occasionally seem, and he wanted to remain so.

Epilogue (2012)

'So did you enjoy the exhibition?'

Faith put the question to Sarah as they seated themselves in an Indian restaurant in North London on a fine summer evening at the end of June. Sarah, who was now a very mature eighteen, had spent the afternoon with her parents at an exhibition of medieval relics in the British Museum. George and Faith had also spent the weekend in London visiting their son Thomas, who now worked for a publishing house in the capital. All six had agreed to meet for a meal.

'I can't say I liked it that much,' Sarah replied. 'Some of the exhibits were beautifully presented, covered in jewels and gold and stuff, but the idea that they might contain the head of John the Baptist, or his blood-soaked hair, or even his tooth, seems a bit sick. Why couldn't they leave the poor man alone?'

Thomas agreed, pointing out that there were, according to the catalogue, which he had studied carefully after visiting the exhibition himself earlier in the week, thirty-six churches dedicated to St.John the Baptist in Constantinople alone. If each of them had a relic (and by the end of the eighth century all altars were required to contain a relic) that would have left them struggling to find anything remotely connected with him.

'I must say I rather liked his tooth,' said George, 'the one displayed in crystal rock originally carved in Cairo. I also liked the note attached to it proclaiming that a dentist had examined it and confirmed that it belonged to a man of about thirty who ate a coarse diet.'

'Well that narrows it down!' Sarah exclaimed. 'It

must be authentic.'

She and Thomas exchanged knowing glances. They always enjoyed teasing their parents about some of their more implausible beliefs.

'I liked the ecumenical significance of the crystal having been carved by Islamic hands,' Faith interjected. 'The idea of treasuring a tooth of a holy man is shared with Buddhism. You know, the tooth of the Buddha in Kandy.'

'I thought candy was bad for teeth,' Thomas joked.

'I find it rather sad,' Philip confessed, 'that people have to preserve objects like this, as if they need something solid that you can point at to give them a sense of security.'

'Why is that sad?' Faith asked. 'If all cultures do it you could argue that it meets a universal need.'

'You could also call it sacramental,' George argued. 'The tooth re-presents, makes present again, the person to whom it belonged.'

'But in many cases it's difficult to connect the gorgeous art object with the relic it contains. That portable altar, for example, that belonged to the Countess of Braunschweig, covered with gems and gilt figures. It is supposed to have contained bits of St.Bartholomew. Well, you know what happened to him: he was flayed alive and then beheaded. When they opened the reliquary bag all they found were fragments of soft tissue.'

'Bits of flayed skin, I suppose,' George suggested.

'But isn't there rather a disparity between the sordid reality of his martyrdom and the rich bejewelled representation of it?'

'Not necessarily,' Faith answered. 'You could say that of the difference between the crucifixion and a crucifix. The latter serves not only as a memorial but a celebration of the salvation brought by the cross.'

163

'Especially when it doesn't have a tortured body on it,' added her husband. 'That distances us from the actual event as well.'

'Do you know I heard a young girl asking for a crucifix in the jeweller's the other day,' Rachel commented. 'She said she didn't want one with a little man on it!'

'One of my students spelt crucifixion with a 'T', as if it were fiction,' Philip sighed. 'And that's one of the few events recorded in the gospels that we can be fairly sure actually happened.'

'That reminds me of something I wanted to ask,' Sarah said. 'Why aren't there more relics associated with Jesus himself?'

'Don't forget that he's supposed to have ascended into heaven,' George replied. 'That doesn't leave much left behind. Mind you, that didn't stop people claiming to have found bits of his umbilical cord and even his foreskin.'

'Don't forget the crown of thorns,' Philip added. 'Brought back from Constantinople to Paris by Louis IX. And all the pieces of the true cross. If they were all authentic there would be enough for a forest.'

'That's how it all began,' George continued. 'All this worship of objects. In the liturgy of Good Friday, venerating the cross on which Christ died.'

'Only we know that it isn't the actual cross,' Philip replied. 'That makes a difference, when we know that our representation is precisely that: a representation. You could say the same about our religious language. It becomes a form of idolatry if we don't recognise the gap between our representations and the real thing.'

'Ah, yes,' Rachel interrupted. 'This is Philip's current crusade. He won't be satisfied until he hears the Pope say that God doesn't exist.'

'I don't want him to say that,' Philip insisted. 'Only

to admit that our ideas about Him are necessarily inadequate. I hate it when people witter on about God as if they knew all about Him,' Philip snapped. 'Or when they talk about Jesus as their "friend".'

'Don't forget we used to be evangelicals ourselves,' Faith reminded him.

'But that was a long time ago. We've grown up since then. It's understandable when young people present Christianity in clear-cut, black and white terms. What I find difficult are older people who have learned nothing along the way, not even humility. It's not just the evangelicals in the Anglican Church; the Catholic Church too is full of fundamentalists who claim absolute certainty about every detail of the faith.'

'But people want certainty,' Rachel commented.

'Then they need to be told that they can't have it,' Philip retorted.

'That's not the most comforting of messages,' Faith observed. 'Not exactly good news.'

'I'm not saying that there isn't a place for doctrine, for attempting to formulate the central tenets of Christianity. I am simply saying that they are complex, not straightforward, not easily grasped. It's a mistake made by fundamentalist atheists as well as evangelicals to think that it's simply a matter of agreeing or disagreeing with a series of propositions.'

'That's all very well,' said Thomas, who had been busily crunching poppodums. 'But the fundamentalists seem to be doing rather well. Some of my friends go to House Churches, groups of believers who meet in halls and schools and have fairly simple beliefs. And they're packed out every week.'

'I suppose there's a freshness about them,' Faith commented. 'They are spreading the good news with all the fervour of the first disciples.'

'And the same first-century world-view,' Philip

added.

'But isn't the message the same as it always was?'

'Yes and no,' Philip argued. 'The same message in a different context becomes different. That's what Newman was trying to say in the *Essay on the Development of Christian Doctrine:* "An idea ...is modified by the state of things in which it is carried out, and depends on the circumstances around it." Christianity grows as it engages with the world, changes as it encounters obstacles.'

Philip was about to embark upon an even longer quotation when he noticed a number of waiters bringing trays laden with the main courses they had ordered. He stopped in his tracks, causing the others to burst into laughter.

'Now shut up and eat your food,' Rachel insisted.

'And be grateful,' Faith added.

'You see,' Philip protested, refusing to be silenced. 'Even the forms of grace have evolved.'

The six of them finally turned their attention to the food and for a while the conversation was only sporadic. Sarah and Thomas began to discuss modern poetry, which was one of the areas which he covered for his publisher. She had recently attended a literary festival in Newcastle in which some of the poets which his firm published had read their work aloud. Thomas admitted that they relied on festivals and readings of this kind to boost sales.

'It sometimes seems as if everyone wanted to write and no-one to read,' he complained. 'There are so many creative writing courses, full of ambitious young writers who bombard us with manuscripts. We try to read them all but it is difficult.'

'They say poetry is the new religion,' Sarah observed.

'They've been saying that for the last two hundred

years,' Philip replied.

'I was taught that departments of English Literature arose to replace the vacuum created by the decline of organised religion.' Thomas, who had studied English at Cambridge, came quickly to Sarah's defence.

'Organised religion isn't completely dead,' his father objected.

'Not yet,' Thomas admitted. 'But you must admit it's pretty moribund.'

'Here perhaps,' Faith acknowledged. 'But not elsewhere in the world. And even here there are signs of life.'

'If your precious Newman is right to see change as a sign of life,' George replied, 'even the Church of England is showing some of those signs. We might even be getting women bishops next month, if the Synod agrees.'

'The mind boggles,' Thomas laughed. 'I might be the first man in England to have a bishop for a mother.'

'You poor thing,' Sarah sympathised, placing her hand on his.

Both sets of parents were intrigued by the obvious chemistry between their offspring. Philip told Rachel later that night as they settled down to sleep that it was a bit like *Wuthering Heights*. It hadn't worked out for Cathy and Heathcliff in the first generation but Hareton and young Cathy had put that right in the end. Maybe Sarah, when she was a bit older, would find happiness with Thomas.

'Isn't he a bit old for her? Rachel objected.

'Well, you never know.'

'No-one ever does,' came the reply.

'That's what I'm always telling you,' Philip insisted.

But Rachel was too tired to argue and the two of them were soon fast asleep.

Acknowledgements

Most of the characters in this novel are fictional. Some, however, such as Dr.Carey, former Archbishop of Canterbury, and Pope John Paul II are historical, having played a part in events to which my fictional characters refer. If my fictional characters show some resemblance to actual people, this is not my intention.

I would like to thank several clergy for sharing some of their own experience with me and explaining the process of training and ordination, in particular the Rev. Helen Arnold, the Rev. Canon Audrey Elkington, and the Rev. Brian McHenry. Any inaccuracy in the novel's representation of this process, of course, should be attributed to me.

The following books are actually discussed in the text: Elisabeth Schüssler Fiorenza, *In Memory of Her: A Feminist Theological Reconstruction of Christian Origins,* Austin Flannery (ed.), *Vatican Council II: The Conciliar and Post-Conciliar Document,* Nicholas Lash, *Theology on Dover Beach,* and Elaine Pagels, *Adam, Eve, and the Serpent.* I have also drawn some material from Christina Rees (ed.), *Voices of This Calling: Experiences of the First Generation of Women Priests.*

There are a number of quotations from John Henry Newman which are acknowledged in the novel itself. Even my subtitle, of course, draws on two of his books: *Callista: A Tale of the Third Century* and *An Essay on the Development of Christian Doctrine.*

I would finally like to thanks my wife Gabriele (who bears no resemblance to any characters in the novel) for reading an early draft and making valuable suggestions for improving it.